The L

"Lee's
execut
sonalit
thinki

"This
and de

Thread Reckoning

"Lee's latest Embroidery Mystery will hook readers with its charming setting and appealing characters. Plenty of spunk and attitude follow Marcy as she solves this well-crafted mystery in a close-knit town full of colorful characters."   —*Romantic Times*

Stitch Me Deadly

"The writing is lively, and the pop culture references abundant. . . . This book should appeal not only to embroidery enthusiasts, antique hunters, and dog lovers, but to anyone who likes a smartly written cozy that neatly ties up all the loose ends surrounding the murder but leaves the reader wanting to know more about the amateur detective, her friends, her life, and her future."   —*Fresh Fiction*

continued . . .

"A well thought-out, free-flowing story that captures your attention and keeps you interested from beginning to end. The comfort of being in a craft store seeps through the pages as Marcy shows her sleuthing side to figure out the town's newest murders."

—The Romance Readers Connection

"There are plenty of threads for readers to pick up, and those who pick up the right thread will have the mystery sewn up in short order."   —The Mystery Reader

The Quick and the Thread

"Lee kicks off a cozy, promising mystery series . . . a fast, pleasant read with prose full of pop culture references and, of course, sharp needlework puns."

—*Publishers Weekly*

"In her debut novel, *The Quick and the Thread*, author Amanda Lee gives her Embroidery Mystery series a rousing start with a fast-paced, intriguing who-done-it that will delight fans of the cozy mystery genre."

—Fresh Fiction

"Stands out with its likable characters and polished plot."   —The Mystery Reader

"If her debut here is any indication, Lee's new series is going to be fun, spunky, and educational. She smoothly interweaves plot with her [main] character's personality and charm, while dropping tantalizing hints of stitching projects and their history. Marcy Singer is young, fun, sharp, and likable. Readers will be looking forward to her future adventures."   —*Romantic Times*

Also by Amanda Lee

The Long Stitch Good Night
Thread Reckoning
Stitch Me Deadly
The Quick and the Thread

THREAD ON ARRIVAL

AN EMBROIDERY MYSTERY

AMANDA LEE

AN OBSIDIAN MYSTERY

OBSIDIAN
Published by New American Library, a division of
Penguin Group (USA) Inc., 375 Hudson Street,
New York, New York 10014, USA
Penguin Group (Canada), 90 Eglinton Avenue East, Suite 700, Toronto,
Ontario M4P 2Y3, Canada (a division of Pearson Penguin Canada Inc.)
Penguin Books Ltd., 80 Strand, London WC2R 0RL, England
Penguin Ireland, 25 St. Stephen's Green, Dublin 2,
Ireland (a division of Penguin Books Ltd.)
Penguin Group (Australia), 250 Camberwell Road, Camberwell, Victoria 3124,
Australia (a division of Pearson Australia Group Pty. Ltd.)
Penguin Books India Pvt. Ltd., 11 Community Centre, Panchsheel Park,
New Delhi - 110 017, India
Penguin Group (NZ), 67 Apollo Drive, Rosedale, Auckland 0632,
New Zealand (a division of Pearson New Zealand Ltd.)
Penguin Books (South Africa) (Pty.) Ltd., 24 Sturdee Avenue,
Rosebank, Johannesburg 2196, South Africa

Penguin Books Ltd., Registered Offices:
80 Strand, London WC2R 0RL, England

First published by Obsidian, an imprint of New American Library,
a division of Penguin Group (USA) Inc.

First Printing, December 2012
10 9 8 7 6 5 4 3 2 1

ALWAYS LEARNING   **PEARSON**

For Tim, Lianna, and Nicholas

Chapter One

It was a gorgeous spring day, and the sun streaming through the windows warmed the back of my neck as I sat on the navy sofa thumbing through Easter patterns. In particular, I was looking for eggs modeled after the famous Fabergé designs. I wanted to make a couple of those—at least, one to send to Mom in San Francisco. Tallulah Falls, Oregon, wasn't all *that* far away from San Fran, but sometimes it felt like it. As if to echo my melancholy mood, Angus—the Irish wolfhound currently lying at my feet, chewing on an unbelievably strong plastic bone—lifted his head and sighed.

I reached down and patted his head. "Cheer up, baby. We'll call Grandma when we get home and see how she's doing."

I don't normally get homesick. I've adjusted very well to my life here on the Oregon coast. I have a beautiful embroidery specialty shop, a lovely home with a fenced backyard, terrific friends, and a couple of wonderful guys who are possibly more than friends.

It was just that Easter was coming up at the end of the month.

Mom had always made such a fuss about Easter when I was growing up. It was second only to Christmas. We'd decorate the house and dye eggs, and Mom would make us new outfits (she's a Hollywood costume designer). And then on the big day, we'd start things off with a scrumptious breakfast before going to church. As soon as we got home from church, she'd hide my Easter eggs and we'd both eat candy from my basket until we were almost sick while I tracked down the eggs. When I was older, we skipped the egg-hiding, but we always had our basket of candy. We'd top the day off by eating a nice dinner and then watching old movies like *Funny Face*, *Gigi*, *Easter Parade*, or *Sabrina*.

The bells over the door jingled. I looked up to see my friend and Tallulah Falls's librarian, Rajani "Reggie" Singh, coming into the shop. She wore a pale blue tunic over matching pants. Several strands of turquoise beads and a few silver bangles rounded out the outfit.

I smiled. "Morning, Reggie! I'm glad you dropped in. Angus and I were feeling a little homesick for San Fran, and you're just what we need to cheer us up."

She raised an index finger. "Hold that thought. I'm getting ready to ask you for a favor."

Angus got up to greet Reggie, and she scratched behind his ears before dropping a kiss onto the top of his head.

As she sat on the sofa beside me, she looked at the Fabergé eggs. "How pretty. You aren't giving yourself much time to make something before Easter, though, are you?"

"Hopefully, it won't be too tough." I frowned slightly. "You said you're here to ask a favor?"

"I am. I've been asked to help with domestic abuse victim assistance at the sheriff's department." Reggie's husband, Manu, is Tallulah Falls's sheriff, so that didn't come as much of a surprise. "Specifically, I'm helping facilitate domestic abuse victims' group therapy and information meetings." She sat down beside me. "I know you've got a full plate, and you're free to say no and I won't be offended in the least. But I'm wondering if you could somehow do an embroidery class for a group of battered women as part of their therapy."

I answered without hesitation. "I was just getting ready to make out a new spring schedule, so I'll do the domestic abuse victims' class in lieu of one of my other weekly classes," I said. "I'll be happy to help."

"Are you sure?" she asked. "The sheriff's department can pay for the materials and give you a small stipend, but it wouldn't be as much as you'd get from offering a paid class on those nights."

"That's fine. I'm honored to be able to help in some way. You say the class is part of their therapy?"

Reggie nodded. "See, most of the victims find it's easier to open up and talk with the other members of the group if their hands are busy and they aren't looking at the others' faces. In the past, group facilitators have used coloring, painting, and working with clay."

"I imagine we'd need something fairly easy," I mused. "Something that would allow the conversation to flow while they were working and something a first-timer could do with ease."

"I agree," Reggie said. "We don't want them to get frustrated. Many have been told repeatedly—some, their entire lives—how incapable or worthless they are."

I shook my head in sympathy. "How about simple stamped cross-stitch and needlepoint projects? That way, the women can work without having to count stitches."

"Sounds great. Plus, it will boost their self-esteem to be able to make something pretty." Reggie smiled and patted my arm. "Thanks. I knew I could count on you. So how are things going with you and Ted?"

Since leaving my accounting job in San Francisco to come here and open my own embroidery shop, the Seven-Year Stitch, there had been two camps with regard to my love life. My best friend, Sadie, who with her husband, Blake, owns MacKenzies' Mochas just down the street, has been pushing me toward a relationship with Todd Calloway, who owns the Brew Crew, a craft brewery and pub across the street. Reggie and Manu, on the other hand, have been encouraging my relationship with Manu's head detective, Ted Nash. Gun-shy after my ex left me at the altar a year before my move to Oregon, I wasn't interested in a serious relationship with either man . . . until recently. I'd begun to see that neither one was mere casual dating material, but I was still having trouble choosing between them.

"Things have been going fairly well," I told Reggie. "Ted and I have been out to dinner a couple times this month, and on Saturday we saw that new thriller with Liam Neeson. It's really good. You and Manu should see it."

"Are things getting serious?" she asked.

"In Liam Neeson's new movie?" I asked, wide-eyed. "Definitely. I'd say things are downright urgent."

"Marcy . . ."

I laughed. "I'm not sure how to answer that, Reggie. I like Ted very much, and I think he feels the same way. We're just taking things slowly. I mean, you know about my past with David . . . and I'm sure you know way more about Ted's past—his divorce, I mean—than I do."

"And what about Todd? Is he in the picture, or is he still dating that waitress from MacKenzies' Mochas?" she asked.

As far as I knew, Todd and Keira had been out only a time or two. But in a small town, word got around, and before you knew it, you were an item. "I don't know about his relationship with Keira," I said, "but he, Sadie, Blake, and I went whale watching last Sunday afternoon."

"You know you're going to have to choose between those two men sooner or later," she said. "Or else somebody's going to get hurt."

"I know." And I did know. I just didn't want to think about it. Not today anyway. Maybe tomorrow. So sue me—I was having a Scarlett O'Hara moment. You didn't have to be in Georgia to have an *I'll think about it tomorrow* moment.

Reggie stood. "I'd better head on back to the library. How soon can you do the first embroidery class for the domestic abuse victims?"

"How soon do you need me?" I asked.

"Well, the first meeting is tonight, but—"

"Then I'd better hurry and get all the materials together," I interrupted.

"No," she said, shaking her head. "That's way too much of an imposition. Just because I got thrown into this last minute doesn't mean you have to start immediately. We'll have an introductory meeting tonight, and I'll tell the group that you've agreed to teach them beginner's cross-stitch and needlepoint and give them an idea of what to expect with regard to the meetings. They'll be happy to know you're going to be doing the class."

"Let's do this then," I said. "I'll try to get everything together. If I can, we'll go ahead and begin the embroidery class tonight. If I can't, I'll bring what I do have, and they can at least get a feel for what they'll be doing." I raised my eyes to the ceiling as I did a mental inventory of what I had on the shelves and in the stockroom in the way of stamped patterns. "How many women are you expecting to attend?"

"At least five," Reggie said. "That's how many are staying at the women's shelter. The local free counseling center has put fliers up that we're forming a support group and will be meeting, so there should be a few more. I'd say to plan on ten to twelve."

"Will they be coming here to the shop?" I asked. "Will we need to provide security?"

"No, they won't be meeting here. The women from the shelter will actually be transported to the library by a van driven by one of Manu's deputies." She shrugged. "It's vital that some of the husbands don't know where their wives are. The other women will come directly to the library."

I bit my lip.

"Are you sure you're up for this?" she asked.

"Of course." At least, I *thought* I was.

After Reggie left, I discovered that I had eight beginner's stamped cross-stitch kits and seven stamped
needlepoint kits, complete with embroidery floss/
yarn and needles. I put them in a tote bag to take to
the library that evening.

Jill, a mannequin resembling Marilyn Monroe who
stands by the cash register at the counter, was wearing fuzzy white bunny ears this morning. No, she
didn't have on the rest of the bunny costume—
Playboy or otherwise—just a pink shift dress I'd embellished with ribbon embroidery—tiny white roses
around the neck, mainly. Since the shop is called the
Seven-Year Stitch, she's sort of the shop mascot . . .
and she's a good way to display some of my work. I
already have embroidery pieces I've completed displayed on the walls and on some of the maple
shelves. And I have pillows featuring my candlewick
handiwork on the two navy sofas that face each other
in the sit-and-stitch square that's set apart from the
merchandise part of store. The rest of the square is
made up of two red club chairs with matching ottomans that also face each other and an oval-shaped
maple coffee table. A red-and-blue braided rug cov-

ers the floor under the table. It's a cozy gathering place.

I started to hang the tote bag on Jill's arm, but I was afraid some customers might come in and want to buy the kits. I took the bag to my office and ordered a dozen of each of the assorted kits from one of my suppliers because the fifteen kits I was taking to the meeting were all I had.

It was Thursday. I typically teach classes on Tuesday, Wednesday, and Thursday evenings, but I'd taken this week off as all my winter classes came to a close the week prior. I had sign-up sheets on the counter for classes in intermediate needlepoint, crewel embroidery, and candlewick embroidery. Since I'd agreed to do the therapy class on Thursday nights for Reggie, my new plan was to choose the classes that were fullest and offer those on the other two class nights. I'd call the people on the other list and offer them either individual instruction or the option to wait to see if the class would have enough people for the following six-week term after these courses were completed.

I stepped back into the shop and looked over the lists. It appeared that intermediate needlepoint was the one that would have to be put on the back burner. I gently pulled at the tape and removed the flier from the countertop. Then I took the flier, my phone, and a notebook to the sit-and-stitch square.

I was notifying the last person on the list when Ted Nash came into the shop, giving my heart a little flutter. He was wearing a blue dress shirt, a navy sport coat, and khakis. I liked seeing him in blue—the color brought out the brilliance of his eyes. I smiled and held up an index finger to indicate I'd be with him in a second. In the meantime, he picked up Angus's tennis ball and the two began a game of fetch.

"I'm really sorry there weren't enough people signed up to warrant a class," I told the woman on the phone. "I'd be happy to offer you some individual instruction, or you can wait and see if the class makes next time."

She told me she'd wait and see if the class would be offered during the summer and said that in the meantime she might stop by the shop with some questions for me on a new project she was starting. I thanked her and hung up.

"Are you crushing hopes this morning?" Ted asked, his lips curling into a wry grin as he took the now-sopping ball from Angus and tossed it again.

I smiled. "Hardly. I just didn't have a lot of interest in one of my classes, so I'm using that night to help out Reggie."

He nodded. "She told me she was going to ask you to do the therapy workshop. Are you sure you're up for that?"

"Sure. I like helping people."

"I know you do," he said, sitting down beside me. "But when you help people, you usually wind up getting in over your head." He took my hand. "It's estimated that over a million women are physically abused by their husbands or partners each year."

"Okay." I drew out the word. "But only about ten or twelve of them will be at the workshop."

He rolled his eyes. "And that's ten or twelve women you will become emotionally attached to and want to protect from their ten to twelve abusive spouses or boyfriends."

"Is that such a bad thing?"

"I just don't want you to get hurt," he said.

"I don't want you to get hurt either, and you put your life on the line every day." I gave him a triumphant little smile.

"It's my job, and I'm trained for it." He studied my face for a second. "Be careful. That's all I ask."

"I will."

"And, please, don't fall in over your head. I mean, your heart is the biggest thing about you, and it's wonderful that you're so caring."

I placed a finger on his lips. "I'll be fine. I appreciate your concern, but I'm only there to teach the women how to embroider. How much trouble can *that* get me into?"

"Ask me that again next week," he said. "Are you free for an early dinner before tonight's meeting?"

"I am."

"Then would you have dinner with me?"

I smiled. "I'd love to."

We planned for Ted to pick me up at my house after I dropped off and fed Angus. Before leaving, he threw the ball for Angus one last time. A well-dressed man who will take the time to play fetch with one's dog is a rare find indeed.

Ted hadn't been gone but about fifteen minutes when Sadie popped in.

"Is everything all right?" she asked, sitting on the sofa beside me.

"Everything is great. Why do you ask?"

"Well, I noticed the sheriff's wife and his head detective heading this way separately but divided only by a short amount of time this morning," Sadie said, stroking Angus's head. "That usually means someone has died around here somewhere."

"Ha-ha. My friends can't simply visit to chat with me?" I held my hand out toward her. "Or to put their aristocratic noses in my business?"

"Touché. . . . Do you really think I have an aristocratic nose?"

"Yes, I do. You have a very regal look about you—I've told you that before."

"I know," she said. "I just never get tired of hearing it."

Sadie was a lovely young woman. She was tall,

had an athletic build, dark brown hair, and eyes that were so brown, they were almost black. Her husband, Blake, had a stocky build, blond hair, and blue eyes. They looked like polar opposites, but they were really a perfect match. I'd known Sadie since she and I had roomed together in college. She had begun dating Blake soon after that, and the two of them had been married for a little more than five years.

"Actually, Reggie did ask me to help her with a very interesting-sounding project," I said. I explained about the embroidery class as a therapy tool. "What do you think?"

"I think you'll be okay as long as you don't get too involved with your students. I mean, it's a wonderful thing to help, and an honor to be asked, but I can just see you going out to round up all these abusers yourself."

I huffed. "Now you sound like Ted."

"Well, Ted is a perceptive guy. He knows—as we all do—that you tend to believe you're ten feet tall and bulletproof rather than a five-foot-tall wimp."

"I am so not a wimp! And I have the free weights in my office to prove it!"

Sadie laughed. "Oh, riiight. The two-pound purple-and-silver dumbbells. I'd forgotten all about those, Xena Warrior Princess."

"I don't know why everyone seems to think I'll get in over my head with these students," I said, with a sigh. "I'm a grown-up. I know I can't save the world."

"But it doesn't stop you from trying. And that's something we all love about you, Marce." She tilted her head, making her long hair spill over her shoulder. "Which reminds me . . . Blake, Todd, and I had a wonderful time whale watching last Sunday."

"Me, too."

"Maybe we can do it again soon," she said. "Or, you know, if Blake and I can't make it, I'm sure you and Todd would have a great time. I mean, when's the last time the two of you went on a date alone?"

"I'm not sure." I really, really did need to make a choice between Todd and Ted soon before the warring factions got out of hand. Reggie was right—someone was going to get hurt if I wasn't careful.

Speaking of Todd, he dropped in about fifteen minutes after Sadie returned to MacKenzies' Mochas. I was finishing up with a customer, so he sat on the sofa and scratched Angus's head while he waited.

When the customer left, and I was sure the other lady browsing in the store wasn't paying attention to Todd and me—well, at least not to *me*; Todd, with his wavy brown hair and chocolate eyes, had gained more than one surreptitious glance from her—I went over and sat on the red club chair.

"Sadie sent you," I said flatly.

He grinned. "Maybe a little."

I arched a brow.

"Okay, okay," he said. "She suggested I drop in and talk with you, but she didn't exactly *send* me. It's not like she's my mom or anything."

"No, she just thinks she's mother hen to both of us. This is about the class, right?"

He glanced up, apparently caught the customer giving him the eye, and gave her a wink. I rolled my eyes. The woman was nearly old enough to be his mother.

"Just being friendly," he whispered. "Might be good for sales."

"Gee, thanks," I whispered back.

"I'm really busy and need to get across the street to work," Todd said. "But why don't you tell me more about this class of yours over dinner tonight?"

"Sorry. I already have plans."

He shook his head slightly. "Sadie warned me that if I'm not careful, somebody else will come in and swoop you off your feet." He watched my expression to see if I'd give anything away.

I struggled to find a proper response to that. Todd was a great guy, but more and more, I found myself thinking about Ted . . . a lot. Ted and I seemed to have more in common, more chemistry . . . more of a chance of having something real. Being unable to find a proper response, I didn't give one. I simply asked him to excuse me so I could check on my customer.

Todd said he'd see me later. The customer—after telling me she'd come back another time—set off after him. It was comical. I could see him talking with her, probably explaining to her that the Brew Crew wasn't open yet. The lady was all smiles and wiggly-fingered waves as she went off down the street.

Had I seen that exchange take place with Ted rather than Todd, it wouldn't have been so cute. It would have irked me . . . made me a little jealous. Of course, Ted wasn't the type to wink at a random woman just to be friendly.

My mind drifted to what I'd wear for our date this evening.

Chapter Two

Ted picked me up at around six o'clock. I'd changed into a pink-and-white floral pencil skirt with a white V-neck sweater. I wore nude pumps, diamond stud earrings, and a diamond pendant. If I'd had time, I'd have curled my short platinum hair just a teensy bit. But I didn't have time, and judging by the smile on Ted's face, I thought I'd done okay anyway.

"You look gorgeous," he said.

"Thank you." He'd changed into black slacks, a white button-down, and a black leather bomber jacket. His hair was still damp from a recent shower, and he smelled fantastic. "You don't look so bad yourself."

"I guess we'd better go since you have to be back at the library by eight."

"And where is it we're going?" I asked.

"Zefferelli's."

"That new Italian place? I'm impressed. Did you have trouble getting reservations?"

"Nope." He winked. "The owner is an old friend. Sometimes it's good to know people in high places."

I linked my arm through his. "Yeah. It really is. Blake and Sadie have been trying to get in for two weeks. Every time they're free, the restaurant is booked."

Zefferelli's was wonderful—from the elegant walnut furniture and pastel blue linens to the Pollo alla Parmigiana to the hazelnut gelato. Even better was the company. I was growing more and more comfortable with Ted—not the kind of comfortable you get from your favorite sneakers, but the kind of comfortable you get from being with someone you totally get and who totally gets you.

I was a little harried but still on cloud nine when I pulled into the parking lot at the library that evening. I'd been afraid I'd be late, but there didn't appear to be any lights on in the building even though Reggie's car was there. I thought maybe Manu had come to take his wife to dinner to thank her for helping out with his domestic abuse victim assistance program. Although there were white rocking chairs on the porch of the Victorian-style house that had been converted into the Tallulah Falls library, the air was cool so I decided to wait in the Jeep.

I nearly jumped out of my skin when someone rapped on my window. I sighed in relief when I saw that it was Reggie. I opened the door, grabbed my purse and the tote containing the embroidery kits, and jumped down out of the Jeep. In case you're wondering, I'd traded the pencil skirt for a pair of jeans before heading over to the library.

"Are you trying to scare me to death?" I asked, as I clicked the remote to lock my doors.

Reggie chuckled. "No. Sorry about that. I just wanted to show you where to come in."

I followed her to the back of the building. She took a key from her pocket and unlocked a door leading to a part of the library I'd never seen. There was a light hanging above a long white folding table, which was flanked by gray metal folding chairs.

"Not the Taj Mahal, I know," Reggie said. "But we have to be extremely careful with these women and take every precaution to ensure their safety and the safety of any children they may bring with them."

"I understand completely." I glanced around the rest of the room. There were shelves lining the walls. Most of the shelves contained old books that needed to be repaired or discarded, but some contained office supplies. There was a countertop that contained snack items and a coffeemaker, and a small refrigerator occupied the corner nearest the door leading into the main part of the library.

"This serves as our all-purpose storage room, break room, party room . . ."

"And hiding place," I finished.

Reggie nodded. "And hiding place." She glanced at her watch. "Officer Dayton is outside helping get students headed in the right direction, and the van from the sheriff's department should be here any minute."

"There's an officer posted outside the library?" I asked. "I didn't see anyone."

"Nope, but she saw you," Reggie said with a smile. "She radioed and told me you were in the parking lot."

I remembered Officer Dayton from the night someone broke into Blake and Sadie MacKenzie's house. She was a pretty, auburn-haired woman with dark green eyes. She'd taken a no-nonsense approach to her job that evening, and I had no doubt she was taking this assignment just as seriously . . . maybe more so.

"Is there anything I can do to help you get things set up?" I asked.

She nodded toward the tote. "Are those the embroidery kits?"

"Yes. I brought fifteen. Do you think that'll be enough?"

"It should be. Let's fan them out across the table," she suggested. She looked at me and then did a double take. "You look awfully cheery tonight—I'd say downright flushed. What have you been up to?"

I blushed. "Nothing. Ted took me to that new Italian place for dinner is all. I'm probably flushed because I thought I'd be late getting here."

"So how *was* Zefferelli's? Or did you notice?"

"I noticed," I said. "It was wonderful."

"And Ted?" Reggie asked.

"Oh, yes. He's wonderful too."

She chuckled. "I was asking what he thought of the restaurant, but I guess that answer says it all." She shook her head slightly. "I'm so glad he's found you. After his divorce, he was so bitter. I was afraid he'd never find the right woman."

I arranged the cross-stitch and needlepoint kits on the table. "What happened to cause the divorce . . . if you don't mind telling me?"

"I don't mind at all. Ted's ex-wife, Jennifer, simply wasn't cut out to be an officer's wife. She couldn't handle his irregular hours or his job hazards."

I frowned. "Was Ted a police officer when they met?"

"Right out of the academy," she said. "So, yes, Jennifer definitely knew what she was getting herself into—or, at least, she *should* have. Maybe she was so taken in with his good looks, charm, personality, magnetism—whatever—that she thought she could convince him to change career paths."

"Was there an impetus that made her realize that was never going to happen?" I asked.

"I think Jennifer decided she wanted to have a baby . . . just not Ted's baby. She didn't want her baby's father to be a policeman. It was *too risky*, she said. *Some criminal could come after our baby. Or you could be killed.*" Reggie scoffed. "I think mainly she just had a whole lot of growing up to do. She got married, realized life wasn't the fairy tale she'd imagined it to be, and then ran out on Ted."

"I'm sorry."

"I was too at the time," she said. "But, even then, as hurt as Ted was, I think her leaving was for the best. He's moved on, and frankly, I think he's happier now than I've ever seen him . . . so far." She winked.

I busied myself with straightening the embroidery kits. Fortunately, the van arrived, and I didn't have to discuss Ted's happiness any further.

The women began filing in. There were five of them. They couldn't have been more different or, yet, more alike. They ranged in age from—given my best guess—eighteen to sixty. Two were well dressed, one was poorly dressed, and the other two appeared to have been clothed with whatever was available at the shelter. I made a mental note to go through my closet to see what I had that I could donate. All of them glanced at Reggie and me and then lowered their heads before taking a seat at the table.

"Hello and welcome," Reggie said in a booming voice. "We're so glad you're here."

No one responded. I noticed the youngest had a black eye and a split lip, and tears sprang to my eyes. I quickly turned away and almost bumped into Officer Dayton.

She gave me a sympathetic nod. "Would you give me a hand with something outside for a sec?"

Not trusting myself to speak, I merely followed her outside.

"It's tough to see these women like this," said Officer Dayton. "But you have to just be glad they're here. They're trying to escape their situation and make better lives for themselves."

"I know," I said. "You're right about it being tough to see, though."

"You don't have to tell me," she said, with a rueful smile. "I've only been on the force for a few months, but already I've seen worse. Are you able to go back in now?"

"Yeah. Thanks."

"No problem." She turned to a woman and a teenage girl who were coming up the path. "Hi, there. The meeting is right through that door. I'm glad you guys could make it."

When the woman and the girl had gone inside, I asked, "Do you know them?"

Officer Dayton nodded. "Yeah . . . they're in a rough situation. That's Mary Cantor and her daughter, Melanie. Mary's husband is abusive not only to her but sometimes to his daughter and his elderly father as well. Mary won't come to the shelter because she's afraid to leave Chester, her father-in-law."

"But isn't there somewhere he could go? A men's shelter?"

"There is," she said. "But it's more of a halfway house. It's no way near as secure as the women's shelter. Besides, she says he needs her and Melanie. And I have no doubt he does."

Officer Dayton stayed outside, and I went back inside. We waited a few more minutes, and another three women joined us before we began.

I had trouble learning everyone's names, mostly because no one talked for the first fifteen or twenty minutes of the meeting other than to give monosyllabic answers to Reggie's questions. After she introduced me to the group, they spoke very little to me other than to tell me what type of embroidery— needlepoint or cross-stitch—they preferred and to choose a kit.

Once everyone had chosen a kit, there were five

left—three cross-stitch and two needlepoint. Reggie took the needlepoint hot-air balloon, and I took the cross-stitch kitten sleeping on a pillow. Working on our own kits allowed Reggie and me to work and to converse with the women without causing anyone to be uncomfortable.

Melanie, Mary Cantor's daughter, was sitting between her mother and a woman named Susan. She had chosen a cross-stitch kit of a long-eared puppy with a bedroom slipper dangling from his teeth. "I like this dog," Melanie said to no one in particular. "He's cute."

"Maybe one day we can have a dog," her mother said.

"I hope so." Melanie sighed.

"I have a dog," I said. "His name is Angus. He's an Irish wolfhound, and he's bigger than I am."

"That's not saying much," said Reggie with a laugh. "But, seriously, when Angus stands on his back paws, he's over six feet tall."

"Wow," Melanie said. "Is he scary?"

"Not at all," I said. "Maybe your mom can bring you by the shop to see him sometime. He loves having visitors!"

"Can we, Mom?" she asked.

"We'll see," Mary said.

"Grandpa wants you to take the tapestry to her shop so she can see how old it is," Melanie said.

"I said we'll see." Mary didn't look up from her needlepoint rose.

I wanted to ask about the tapestry, but I didn't want to cause Mary—or especially Melanie—any discomfort. I waited until after the class and spoke with Mary discreetly.

"What sort of tapestry was Melanie talking about?" I asked.

Mary gave me a half shrug. "Pop has this piece of embroidered cloth that he thinks is a treasure map. Frankly, I don't even think it's that old, but he thinks it's an antique and that it could be the answer to our prayers. When I told him about class tonight, he got really excited and wanted me to show you the tapestry so you could confirm how old it is."

"I could probably look at it and tell you," I said. "I'm really good with textiles."

"I'd rather you look at it and tell *him*," Mary said. "If you could convince him that it's not what he believes it to be—some ancient treasure map—then maybe he'd leave with us, and Melanie and I could get out of that house. As it is, he won't budge."

"Why not?" Reggie asked. "I'm sorry. I didn't mean to eavesdrop—but I couldn't help overhearing. Your father-in-law is an adult of legal age and of good mental capacity, isn't he?"

Mary nodded. "But he keeps telling me he has a plan. He believes that this grand scheme of his is about to come together and that he, Mel, and I can go far away where Adam will never find us . . . at least, until Adam comes to his senses and agrees to get help . . . which—if he honestly thinks Adam will ever do that—makes me question Pop's mental capacity."

"He just hopes, Mom," Melanie said quietly. "I do too. I love Dad. He gets upset sometimes . . . that's all."

"Pop encourages us to go on without him, but I'm afraid to leave him there alone with Adam." Mary raised her eyes to Reggie's. "Will you visit with Pop . . . see if you can talk some sense into him? If you could persuade him to leave, we could go tomorrow."

Reggie put her needlepoint kit down on the table, removed her glasses, and pinched the bridge of her nose. "What if Adam sees me? He knows I'm Manu's wife. He'll know something's up." She lowered her hand. "I'll be happy to call Chester and speak with him over the phone."

"That won't work," Mary said. "He doesn't hear well over the phone. He doesn't hear well at all, for that matter, but in person, he can lip-read."

"Adam doesn't know me," I said. "I wouldn't mind going and checking out the tapestry. Maybe if Chester learns it isn't authentic, he'll decide to go with you."

Mary shook her head. "According to Pop, Adam doesn't know about the tapestry."

"Then I won't go as an embroidery shop owner." I mulled this over for a second, wondering what my excuse would be. Door-to-door salesperson? No, there aren't that many of those around anymore. Census taker? Charitable donation seeker? Then it came to me. "Reggie, doesn't the library have a book-mobile? If so, couldn't we use that?"

"We do have one," Reggie said.

"What's a bookmobile?" Melanie asked.

"It's someone who delivers books to shut-ins," I said, my gaze encompassing her, her mother, and Reggie. "A bookmobile would provide me with a legitimate excuse to be there, and if Adam is at home, then I can actually talk with Chester about books. When I come back with the books he'd like to read, then maybe Adam won't be there."

"That could work," Mary said. "Chester loves to read . . . especially old history and shipwreck books."

"What do you think, Reggie?" I asked.

Reggie hesitated, and I could tell she was struggling.

"It'll be fine," I continued. "I won't be pushy. If Adam won't allow me into the house, then I'll leave."

"Dad usually leaves for work at seven in the morning," Melanie said. "Mom doesn't leave until eight. If you got there just after Dad left and were gone before he comes back home at lunchtime, it should be okay."

I looked at Reggie. "What do you think?"

Reggie blew out a breath. "I don't like it, but if you're game—and if Mary and Melanie think it will help get them all to safety—then we'll do it." She bit her lip. "Let's just not tell Ted until after the fact."

After class, Reggie and I went to MacKenzies' Mochas to work out all the details of our plan. Sadie greeted us at the door and escorted us to a table in the corner.

"How did the class go?" she asked.

"It went fine," Reggie said. "Thanks for asking. How about a decaf latte, please, with extra whipped cream?"

"Sure. Marcy?" Sadie asked.

"I'll have the same."

With a nod, Sadie hurried off to get our drinks. I knew she had wanted to hear about the meeting in more satisfying detail, but Reggie and I needed to hammer out our plan and get home—her to Manu, and me to Angus. Besides, Sadie could rest assured that I'd tell her everything tomorrow.

"The library does have a bookmobile," Reggie said. "But I'm driving."

Sadie returned with our lattes, gave me another odd look, and then left.

"But what if Adam Cantor sees you driving the van?" I asked. "Won't he find it suspicious that the library director is doing her own grunt work?"

"Of course not," she said. "What could be more natural than a librarian driving a bookmobile? Besides, there's no way I'm letting you go to the Cantor place by yourself. Adam has an assault record a mile long. He's been sentenced to anger management sessions twice, and he served a year in county lockup for assault with a deadly weapon when Melanie was still in elementary school. But none of that seems to help."

"I'm so sorry for Mary and Melanie," I said. "They seem sweet."

"They are," Reggie said. "I've never met Chester, but he doesn't appear to be anything like his son."

"Isn't that unusual?" I asked. "I thought abuse typically ran in families."

"It does. From what I've heard, Adam suffered his abuse at the hands of his stepfather. Chester and Adam's mother divorced when Adam was still a baby. I don't think Chester made the most of his time with his son until Adam was in his early teens." She shook her head. "By then, the damage had already been done."

As I sipped my latte, I thought about what Reggie had said about Adam. His jail sentence and anger management classes had apparently not mellowed him out much. "Adam must be pretty mean."

"He is," Reggie said. "But he can be charming too. Otherwise, Mary never would have fallen for him."

I nodded. Charming or not, if this man found out we were duping him, he was going to be furious.

Reggie looked at her watch. "I've got to run. I'll pick you up in the morning between seven and seven fifteen."

"All right. See you then."

Reggie's chair hadn't got cold before Sadie slid into it. "Okay. Spill."

"Spill what?" I asked, merely prolonging the inevitable.

"Tell me what you and Reggie are up to," she said. "I thought I heard the name Adam Cantor mentioned."

"She and I need to talk with Adam's father, so we're going to the house under the guise of a bookmobile visit," I said. "It's no big deal."

"It *is* a big deal," she insisted. "Adam Cantor is bad news." She turned and motioned for Blake.

"What's up?" Blake asked, arriving at our table while drying his hands on his black apron.

"Marcy is going to Adam Cantor's house in the morning," Sadie said.

Blake's eyes widened. "What? No way." He pulled up a chair and sat down.

I blew out a breath. "It's not that big a deal, guys. Reggie and I are going by the house tomorrow after Adam has left for work. If anyone sees us there, we'll look like we're just the friendly, neighborhood book-mobile."

"And what if Adam or the neighbors want to know why you didn't visit any *other* houses?" Blake asked.

"I hadn't thought of that," Sadie said.

Actually, I hadn't either, so I scrambled for an answer. "The reason we're only visiting the Cantors' house is . . . because patrons have to sign up for the service at the library and give Reggie their information there." I nodded, satisfied that my explanation sounded reasonable. "We can say Mary put her father-in-law on the program because he's a shut-in who enjoys reading."

They both simply looked at me, making me feel as if I were their reckless teenage daughter and they were my parents. Even though we were all three fairly close in age, they had always treated me as if I were their baby sister.

"I'll be fine," I said. "Reggie will be there."

"Why are you going there in the first place?" Blake asked.

"Mary wanted Reggie to talk with her father-in-law about leaving with her and Melanie—Mary and Adam's daughter," I said.

"Then why are *you* going?" Sadie asked.

"Because Chester—the father-in-law—wants me to determine the authenticity of a tapestry he believes to be an antique." I shrugged. "Reggie will work everything out to where we'll be safe. I trust her."

"I trust her too," Blake said. "But she's no match for Adam Cantor. Did you know he's served jail time for assault?"

I nodded. "Reggie told me about it."

"Did she tell you that he committed this assault at the Brew Crew and that he did over five thousand dollars' worth of damage to Todd's bar with a baseball bat?" he asked.

"No." I had a feeling I'd be getting a call from Todd later and that he too would try to convince me not to go to the Cantor house tomorrow morning. "I can't bail on Reggie—or Mary and Melanie—at this point. Adam Cantor has no reason to be suspicious of me . . . no reason to harm me. . . . I'm merely delivering library books to his father."

"And trying to convince his father, his wife, and his daughter to leave him," Sadie said.

"Not the wife and daughter," I said. "They're already poised for flight. They just don't want to leave the poor old guy there to fend for himself."

Sadie squeezed my hand. "Promise me you'll be careful . . . and that this will be a onetime thing and that you won't get in over your head."

"I promise." And when I said it, I had every intention of keeping that promise.

Chapter Three

I'd just let Angus out into our fenced backyard when Reggie arrived the next morning. I was surprised to see that Officer Dayton was with her.

"Good morning, Ms. Singer," Officer Dayton said.

"Please, call me Marcy," I said.

"Then, please, call me Audrey," she said with a smile. She was dressed casually in black slacks, a bulky black sweater, and black flats. Noticing me looking at her clothes, she asked, "Are you wondering about my husky ninja costume?"

I inclined my head. "Maybe a little."

She pulled up her right pant leg to reveal an ankle holster with a small gun. Then she turned and slightly raised her sweater so I could see the Taser located at the small of her back. "I'm not expecting any trouble, but I'm prepared if there is any."

After getting the lecture last night from Sadie and

Blake about the dangers of Adam Cantor, I was glad to see that Officer Dayton—Audrey—had our backs. Surprisingly, I hadn't heard from Todd last night. I didn't know whether Sadie had been unable to reach him or it had been too late when he'd finished up at the Brew Crew to call me and add his two cents to the Adam Cantor warning.

Reggie looked at her watch. "We should be moving along. Marcy, Audrey will be in the back of the van out of sight."

I grinned. "I feel like we're going on a secret undercover mission."

"I'll agree it's kind of exciting," Reggie said. "Usually, it's Manu who gets to do all the fun stuff."

"It won't be fun if we have a confrontation with Mr. Cantor," Audrey said.

Reggie and I glanced at each other. I knew we were both thinking that it might be fun to see Audrey spring into supercop mode.

When we arrived at the Cantor residence, a handsome man who appeared to be in his late thirties was pulling away from the curb in a white late-model SUV.

"Oh, crap," I mumbled.

"It'll be all right," Reggie said.

The man in the SUV circled around and came back to see what we were doing. He pulled up beside the van and put his window down. "What are you doing here?" His question sounded more curious than demanding, but there was an undercurrent of steel that warned that Adam Cantor was not a man to be crossed.

Reggie lowered the driver's-side window of the van. "Good morning, Mr. Cantor. We're here to see your father."

"What do you want with him?"

"We've brought him a selection of books we thought might interest him." She glanced down and rifled through a couple blank papers. "It says here he likes nonfiction . . . history?"

"Yeah." He smiled, showing even white teeth. "Yeah, he does. It's pretty early for a delivery, though, isn't it?"

"It is," Reggie agreed. "I don't like the bookmobile to interfere with regular library operations, so we typically run it before and after library hours."

Adam squinted into the van at me. "You don't look all that familiar to me. I don't think I've seen you at the library before."

"I'm not an actual employee," I said. "I'm just here to help Reggie this morning. I have an embroidery shop in town, so I don't have to go to work until ten a.m."

"Nice of you to give up your morning like this," Adam said.

I smiled. "I think it's important that everybody

has access to books. Besides, it's only a couple days a week. I can spare that."

He nodded. "So you brought books to show to Dad? I'll go back inside with you. There might be something there I'd like to read."

"Of course," Reggie said.

This was not in the plan. She and I were both smiling, but I knew her mind had to be racing even faster than mine was. We needed to get rid of Adam Cantor, or else our intended conversations would never take place. But if we tried to get rid of him, he'd be more suspicious than he probably already was and would never allow us into his home.

"I'll start grabbing the books," I said to Reggie, hopefully giving Audrey time to hide before I opened the van's back door.

"Be right there," Reggie said, taking out a pen and scribbling on one of the blank papers before placing it in a folder.

I hopped out of the van, went around to the back, and opened up the door. I saw Audrey standing just to the side of a small cart filled with books.

"Take the entire cart," she whispered.

By that time, Reggie had joined me.

"Can you grab that end?" I asked, getting the handle of the cart closest to me.

"Of course," she said, her sunny affect never wavering.

We'd barely had time to shut the door before Adam Cantor came around Reggie's side of the van.

"So these are the books?" he asked, craning his neck to read the titles.

"These are all we have this trip," Reggie answered. "If there's something specific you'd like, I can put in a request and hopefully we'll be able to bring it to you next time."

"All right. Can you two manage that cart okay?" he asked.

"Sure," I said.

He checked his watch. "I'll run back into the house for a second, but then I need to get to work. Maybe the next time you come, it won't be such a surprise."

Reggie and I got the cart up onto the curb as Adam Cantor jogged up the sidewalk and into the house.

Adam graciously held the door open for us and invited us in. "Pop!" he called, over his shoulder. "You'd better get out here. There are some mighty pretty ladies here to see you!" He winked at us. "He's just finishing up his breakfast. He'll be right with you. In the meantime, make yourselves at home here in the living room."

From the corner of my eye, I noticed Mary just inside the door nervously fingering the hem of her gray cardigan.

Adam turned toward her. "Mary, don't just stand there. Come and introduce yourself."

"We've met," Reggie said. "Remember, Mrs. Cantor, when you signed your father-in-law up for the bookmobile delivery?"

"Oh, of course. It's good to see you." Mary said.

I held out my hand. "Hi, Mrs. Cantor. I'm Marcy Singer. I don't work for the library, but I'm helping Reggie out this morning."

Mary shook my hand.

"Why didn't you tell me we had company coming this morning, Mary? I'd have called in and said I'd be late for work." Adam was smiling, but his eyes and his voice were like flint. He looked at his watch before shooting an accusatory glare at Mary.

Mary glanced up at her husband and then down at the floor. "I'm sorry, Adam. I must've forgotten about it."

"Yes, you must have. If I don't go on, I'll be late." He turned back to Reggie and me. "It was a pleasure meeting you, Ms. Singer. Mrs. Singh, I appreciate your kindness to my father."

"Anytime," Reggie said.

I wheeled the cart farther into the living room. "Mrs. Cantor, would you care to take a look at the books we brought for your father-in-law to choose from?"

Mary stood staring at the door, watching Adam

stride down the sidewalk. She raised her hand and waved slightly, but I doubt he saw her. When at last his vehicle roared away, she visibly relaxed.

"I'm sorry," Reggie said. "We thought he'd be gone before now. Are you in trouble?"

Mary nodded. "A little. It's probably not that bad, though . . . nothing I can't handle. Besides, hopefully, I won't be here to face his wrath when he gets home." A metallic scraping sound from the kitchen nabbed her attention, and she hurried into the other room. "Coming, Pop. Let me help you."

"I don't need any help," Chester Cantor said, struggling to get his walker through the narrow door leading from the kitchen to the living room. He smiled when he saw Reggie and me. "Well, hello there. To what do I owe this honor?"

I loved him on sight. He was short—almost as short as me—and rather square. He kind of reminded me of the elderly man in the animated movie *Up*.

Reggie did a quick check over her shoulder to make sure Adam Cantor hadn't doubled back on us. "We're here to bring you some books. We'd also like to talk with you about letting us get you, Mary, and Melanie to safety."

He raised a hand and flicked his wrist as if he were shooing away a fly. "I've got a plan. Soon I'm going to be able to get us all somewhere safe . . . and then we'll make Adam get some help so he won't lose his entire family like I did once."

"I hear you have a tapestry you'd like for me to look at," I said.

His face brightened. "You're the gal from the embroidery shop?"

"That's me."

"Seen many tapestries, have you?" His eyes were sparkling with excitement.

"I've seen quite a few," I said. "You might even say I'm an expert on old tapestries."

He grinned. "Come with me, young lady." He looked around at Mary and Reggie. "You two stay here."

"Melanie and I have to leave soon," Mary said, "or else she and I are going to be late for school and work."

"Well, you two go on and do what you need to do," Chester said. "I'll be fine with . . . What's your name?"

"Marcy," I answered.

"I'll be just fine with Marcy here." He jerked his head toward the door leading to the narrow hallway. "Let's go."

I shot a look at Reggie, and she gave me a combination shrug-slash-nod that I guessed meant I should go with Mr. Cantor, check out the tapestry, and get the lowdown on his plan.

As I followed Mr. Cantor down the tight hallway, Melanie burst through her bedroom door, kissed the man on the cheek, and said, "Bye, Grandpa! See you later! Bye, Marcy!"

Mr. Cantor shook his head. "Always in a rush, that one. Oh, well, it's good to hurry while you've got some hurry left in you, I reckon." He opened a door at the end of the hall to reveal a small bedroom. The room had a full-sized four-poster bed, an oak dresser and the matching chest of drawers, a navy blue recliner that had seen better days, and a TV that was mounted in the corner of the room across from the bed and the recliner. The room smelled of menthol muscle rub, and I imagined Mr. Cantor spent much of his time in this tiny place. I looked around for the tapestry he'd spoken of, but the walls were bare with the exception of a few framed family photographs.

He gestured toward the neatly made bed. "Have a seat there on the foot of the bed—or in the recliner if you'd rather—while I get the tapestry."

I didn't want to mess up the bed, so I perched on the edge of the recliner. Mr. Cantor opened the bottom drawer of the dresser, emptied the socks, scarves, and gloves it contained onto the bed, and flipped it over. Taped to the bottom of the drawer was a large manila envelope. He carefully removed the tapestry from the envelope, unfolded and smoothed it out on the bed where I could see it.

The tapestry appeared to be an ancient map of the Oregon coast. Besides Tallulah Falls, I recognized the names Lincoln City, Coos Bay, and Waldport. Near Tallulah Falls, there was the depiction of a schooner sinking into the ocean. Beneath the ship was the name *Delia*. And beneath the ship's name was an X.

"It's gorgeous," I said. The background was dark brown wool. Dark wools were often indicative of textiles from the Civil War era. "It must be well over a hundred years old." As I said it I realized Mary would be disappointed I had confirmed it was an antique. Still, I couldn't deny the truth of that.

"It sure is." Mr. Cantor tapped the X. "And look here. It's a treasure map."

I was trying to humor him, but I didn't see how he'd decided that this tapestry was a *real* treasure map. "It does remind you of a treasure map, doesn't it? May I pick it up?"

He nodded.

I took the tapestry and held it closer to the light. There were no holes, little wear and tear on the bindings and edges, and only a couple of tiny stains. I turned the cloth over, but there was nothing on the back except the work that made the beautiful map on the front.

"You don't believe it's a map, do you?" Chester asked. "Let me explain. My great-grandmother was a Ramsay."

I nodded slowly, still having no idea where he was going with his story and not sure he had a clue himself. I carefully placed the tapestry back onto the bed.

He pushed his walker out of the way and sat down beside the tapestry. "The Clatsop Indians used to tell stories about Jack and George Ramsay. Jack had fair skin, red hair, and freckles. They were the children of an English sailor and a Clatsop woman."

"And you believe your great-grandmother was related to these people?"

"Indeed I do," he said. "Mother said Grandmother Wells—she was born a Ramsay, married a Wells—had the prettiest head of red hair you ever did see. And I believe she made this tapestry after years of hearing her parents talk about this shipwreck off the coast of Tallulah Falls." He studied the delicate fabric. "They lived up in Vancouver, and I believe Grandmother made this tapestry in the hope that one day she or one of her children would return to the Oregon coast and find that treasure."

I reached over and gently placed my hand on his arm. "Mr. Cantor, don't you think someone would've found it by now?"

"Treasures are still being discovered every day, Marcy." He looked up at me. "Oh, I see what you're saying. You're thinking I'm too old to be searching the seas for treasure."

"I'm not saying that at all. I just don't think it's the solution to your current problem."

"It couldn't hurt. Adam and Mary are always fighting about money. There's never enough. He thinks she mismanages it, but she does the best she can." He smiled sadly. "I am old. And I'm out of ideas. But I've been in touch with a treasure hunter, and he thinks there could be something of the *Delia* left for us to find. As late as July of 2010, gold coins and a bronze cannon from a 1715 shipwreck were found off the coast of Florida."

"But, Mr. Cantor, you and Mary and Melanie need to get to safety now. You can *still* locate the treasure," I said. "Take the tapestry with you."

"And let someone *steal* it from me at that *homeless* shelter? Steal the tapestry *and* the treasure?" He shook his head in obvious alarm.

"Then give it to someone you trust to hold on to it . . . your attorney, maybe. Or put it in a safe-deposit box."

He sighed. "They want to leave, don't they? Mary and Melanie, I mean."

I nodded. "They want to do it today . . . and they want you to go with them, Mr. Cantor. In fact, they won't leave without you. They're afraid for you to stay here with your son alone."

"I'm getting what I deserve," he said, his rheumy eyes filling with tears. "I did Adam wrong all those years ago when I divorced his mother. Then his mother married a man who was harsh with Adam. I later tried to make it up to him, but for the longest time, Adam wouldn't have anything to do with me. And who could blame him?" He lowered his head. "This treasure could be the answer to my prayers. It could let me get my daughter-in-law and my grand-child to a safer place, and then Adam would see what he was missing. He'd understand what he's been doing to them. And then I could convince him to let me get him some help."

I patted his hand. "I hope you do find that trea-sure, Mr. Cantor."

"Will you help me?" he asked, raising his eyes to mine.

"If I can," I said.

"Will you take the tapestry somewhere safe for me? If you'll take it to the bank, or to the police station—anywhere they'll put it under lock and key, I'll go. Then when Mary, Melanie, and I get to a safe place, you can get it back for me. What do you say?"

How could I say *no*?

Chapter Four

We still had a little time before any of us had to be at work, so Reggie, Audrey, and I went to MacKenzies' Mochas. Keira seated us—which made me uncomfortable since she despised me—and took our orders. I requested my usual low-fat vanilla latte with a dash of cinnamon, Reggie ordered a cappuccino, and Audrey went with Colombian dark roast coffee with cream and sugar.

As soon as Keira had sauntered away from our table, I leaned in so I could lower my voice. "Do you think they'll go through with it? I'm still afraid Mr. Cantor might back out at the last minute."

"Well, Manu said he'd send two plainclothes deputies in an unmarked car to pick Mr. Cantor up first," Reggie said quietly. "The officers will take him to the men's shelter before going to pick Mary up at work.

From there, they'll take Mary and collect Melanie from school."

"Mary did say she'd take an early lunch so she can come home and pack up some things for herself and Melanie, right?" Audrey asked.

"Right." Reggie sighed. "Mr. Cantor was supposed to start packing as soon as we left."

"I think he will," I said. "He's kinda like a little boy, though. He made me promise to hold on to that tapestry he had and not to show it to anyone. He thinks it's a treasure map and that it'll lead to enough money to fix all his family's financial problems." I looked up to see Keira standing there with our drinks.

"So, where's this treasure supposed to be?" she asked, distributing our coffees.

I shrugged, wishing I hadn't mentioned the tapestry here in public. Mr. Cantor had trusted me with his secret, and I'd already inadvertently revealed it to a woman who considered me her rival for Todd's affections. And I had no idea whom she might tell. "I seriously doubt there is a treasure. The person who told me about it is simply a sad old man who's looking for a miracle."

"Aren't we all?" Audrey said. "Looking for a miracle, I mean." She looked at Keira. "Could we get some extra napkins, please?"

With a frown, Keira hurried to the counter, grabbed some napkins, came back and plunked them in the center of our table before flouncing away again.

Audrey smiled at me. "Clearing rubberneckers away from crime scenes is one of my specialties. Did you know that?"

"I do now," I said with a grin.

"As for Mr. Cantor," she said, "maybe he'll get his wish. I hope so. It really is an old tapestry. I'm not saying it's a treasure map, by any stretch of the imagination, but . . ."

"Hey, you never know," Reggie said. "I'd love to see this whole situation—the family gathering the courage to leave—be a wake-up call to Adam Cantor so that he decides to become the husband, father, and son his family needs."

I went home to get Angus before opening the shop. We'd just been at the Seven-Year Stitch for a moment—I hadn't even had time to hang my jacket in my office—when Sadie rushed in.

"What's this I hear about a treasure map?" she asked.

I groaned. "Oh, no. That ignorant, spiteful Keira! What did she say?"

"She said you were talking about someone giving you a treasure map for safekeeping." Sadie sat down on the sofa facing the street. "She said it's rumored to be a treasure worth millions."

I let out a growl of frustration as I stormed into my office, hung my jacket on the coatrack, and put my purse and tote bag under the desk. Angus retreated to his bed under the counter in the shop.

"Does that reaction mean it's true?" Sadie called.

"No!" I came out of the office and stooped by Angus's bed. "I'm sorry, baby." I stroked his head. "I'm not angry with you."

He wagged his tail but stayed where he was.

I straightened and went to sit beside Sadie. "You know what this is, don't you?" I asked. "This is Keira's attempt to have me inundated with treasure hunters. I told her there wasn't a treasure."

"Is there?"

"I seriously doubt it." I explained about my visit with Mr. Cantor, his showing me the tapestry, and his hope that it would prove to be a map that would lead him to a treasure that would help solve all his family's woes. "It's an old tapestry. His mother probably used to entertain him with stories of pirates and treasure when he was a little boy. And now that he's . . . well . . . in his second childhood, he's returned to those dreams because he sees no other alternative to his family's money problems. I guess he figures it makes about as much sense—maybe more so—as the lottery."

"Well, gee . . . that's sad," Sadie said.

"It is. You'd love this little old guy, Sadie. I wanted to adopt him and bring him home with me." Tears pricked the backs of my eyes. "He says he deserves for his son to mistreat him. But he doesn't. He's a dear, sweet man." I blinked back the tears and sniffled. "I'm going to take another look at that tapestry, too. If there's any way it *is* a treasure map, I'll help him find that treasure."

Sadie sighed. "You started that class—what—last night?"

I nodded.

"I knew you'd get in over your head with this group before everything was said and done, but this has to be a record even for you."

That afternoon I was in my office looking up Fabergé eggs on the computer. I wanted to make something unique for Mom . . . and that meant finding a good enough photograph that I could use to create a pattern. I learned that most of the famous Fabergé eggs were miniatures that could be worn on chains but that it was the larger ones created for Alexander and Nicholas that were the most popular. I lucked out and found a site that had a list of the Tsar Imperial Easter eggs and a link to photographs of some of them.

The one I decided to make for Mom was the Rose Trellis egg. It had a pale green background with baby pink roses and golden branches sporting darker green leaves. The trellis was silver and inlaid with tiny diamonds. I could put glass beads on the trellis to make the piece sparkle like the original. I uploaded the image into my cross-stitch pattern-making software. The many minute color variations that had been undetectable in the photograph but that had been picked up by the software made the pattern far too complex. I'd need to figure out a way to simplify the pattern before embarking on the project.

The bells over the door indicated I had a visitor.

"Coming!" I called, getting up and hurrying into the shop.

My visitor was Ted. Angus had already dropped a tennis ball at his feet, and Ted was scratching the dog behind the ears.

I smiled. "Hi, there." He looked handsome in his dark gray suit and crisp white shirt. My gaze traveled from his cobalt eyes to his unsmiling lips, and my own smile faded. "Uh-oh. I don't like that look. What's wrong?"

He straightened, blew out a breath, and remained silent.

"Ted, please. . . . It's the Cantors, isn't it? Did something happen?"

He nodded. "When deputies arrived at the home

to escort Mr. Cantor to the shelter, there was no response to their repeated knocking."

I started shaking my head. "No . . ."

"Chester Cantor is dead, Marcy."

I let out a wail, and Ted quickly bridged the distance between us and gathered me into his arms. He walked me back into the office and sat me down in the desk chair. He knelt in front of me, holding both my hands.

"How . . . ? How did they find him?" I asked. "Was it his heart? Had he fallen after we left? I knew someone should've stayed there and helped him pack. *I* should've stayed."

"No, Marcy. It wasn't any of those things. He . . . The deputies found him lying on the sofa in the living room with a book on Oregon shipwrecks beside him." His eyes shifted from mine to our clasped hands. "His neck was broken."

I gasped and then sobbed harder. "He . . . was . . . *murdered*?"

Ted stood, lifted me out of the chair, sat back down, and settled me onto his lap. I clung to him and cried until my sobs had diminished into quiet tears.

"This is my fault," I whispered.

"It's not," Ted said.

"Yes, it is. I mentioned in MacKenzies' Mochas that Mr. Cantor had what he believed was a treasure map, and someone killed him over it."

"That's not what happened."

"Do you know that for sure?" I asked. "Do you have the person in custody? Did he say he killed Chester Cantor for some other reason? Did Adam come home and catch him packing? Had the house been robbed?"

"We don't have anyone in custody." He shifted his eyes. "The house appeared to have been ransacked, but . . ."

I cried out in frustration and anger. This was my own fault, but part of the blame rested on that big-mouthed Keira.

Suddenly, we were moving. Ted was rolling the chair with us in it over to the mini-fridge. He opened the door, took out a bottle of water, and handed it to me.

"Drink. You've cried so much, I'm afraid you'll dehydrate," he said.

"Thank you." I twisted the cap off the bottle and took a long drink. I immediately began to hiccup.

Ted tried to suppress a smile. "You need some sugar."

My eyes dropped to his lips. It probably would help, but I thought Ted's timing was a little off.

He rolled us over to the coffeepot, reached over my head, and took a packet of artificial sweetener from the tray that held the creamer and sweetener packets. "You don't have any real sugar?"

I shook my head.

He handed the sweetener to me. "This might still work. Open it and swallow the contents."

I looked at the packet and then back at Ted with a frown.

"Trust me," he said. "It works. Usually."

I tore off the corner of the packet of sweetener, swallowed the contents, and my hiccups immediately abated. I raised my eyebrows. "It worked. It really worked."

"You see? I'm good for what ails you," he said with a wink.

I smiled slightly. "Yes, you are. You really are."

"For the record, I don't know what Mr. Cantor's assailant was looking for, but I highly doubt it was a treasure map."

"Did he suffer?" I asked quietly.

"It appeared he'd dozed off while reading. The coroner doesn't think Mr. Cantor ever woke up," Ted said.

"I hope he didn't. And I hope he was having a wonderful dream. Maybe he was dreaming he'd found the treasure." I set the water bottle on the counter by the coffee tray. "He asked me to hold on to the tapestry for safekeeping. May I photograph it before I turn it over to you?"

"Of course. But, again, Marce, I don't think that's why he was killed."

"You said the house was robbed," I said.

"I said it *appeared* to be. We don't know what, if anything, is missing yet. Adam and Mary Cantor will have to tell us that."

I closed my eyes. "What about Mary?" My eyes flew open. "And Melanie? Will they still go to the shelter? What will happen?"

"Manu and the domestic abuse victim assistance supervisor talked with Mary before advising Adam of his father's death," said Ted. "I believe Mary has decided to stay in the home for now. She can't imagine leaving Adam just after his father died. But if she and Melanie have any problems, they're going to call Manu. He'll protect them."

"I know." I hugged him. "Thank you for coming to tell me in person."

"You're welcome. I knew you'd be upset, and I wouldn't have had you find out any other way."

I pulled back and looked at his handsome face. Our eyes locked as I caressed his cheek with my palm. When my eyes lowered to his full lips this time, he leaned forward and kissed me. I buried my hands in his hair as I brought him as close as I could. His kiss felt so good . . . so right.

"Hey, are . . ."

Ted and I came up for air at the sound of Todd's voice. He was standing in the doorway.

"Sorry I interrupted," he said, turning to leave.

I started to call out to him, but I didn't. Even though this was not how I'd intended to make my choice, it was made. It actually *had* been made for quite some time. I wanted to give a relationship with Ted a shot. I'd talk with Todd later . . . if he was still speaking with me.

"You okay?" Ted said.

I nodded. "I am. Are you?"

"I'm great. This is what I've been waiting for," he said. "*You* are who I've been waiting for."

"Ditto." I kissed him again before standing. "Let me get you that tapestry."

Chapter Five

After Ted left, I called Sadie and asked her if she could watch Angus and the shop for about fifteen minutes.

"Sure," she said. "Is anything wrong?"

"I just need to run over to the Brew Crew and talk with Todd for a second," I said.

"Oh, okay. I'll be right there!"

I suspected that chipper note in her voice would fade after she found out what I was going to talk with Todd about.

Minutes later, Sadie—face beaming—came practically skipping into the Seven-Year Stitch. I was sitting on one of the red club chairs, puzzling over the Fabergé egg pattern. She sat on the navy sofa facing the window and peered at my pattern.

"That's pretty," she said. "Looks hard, though. Are you going to the Brew Crew to see if Todd can give you a shot of courage before you start on that?"

"Actually, I need to modify this pattern to make it simpler," I said.

She leaned forward and squinted at me. "You've been crying."

I ignored her observation for the moment. "I'm going to talk with Todd because he walked in on Ted and me kissing a few minutes ago."

Sadie's silence drew my eyes over to her face. She was gaping at me. "Is that why you've been crying? Because you think this has cost you your chance with Todd?"

"No. I'm sorry Todd found out the way he did, but I've made my choice," I said. "I believe Ted is the right guy for me."

"Oh." The sound was small, yet somehow accusatory. "Then I guess this is my fault."

"How do you figure that?" I asked.

"I told Todd about Keira and the treasure map fiasco. That's why he came to see you. Have you had treasure seekers bugging you all day?"

I shook my head. "I had a few calls, but no one has been here. Someone did break into Chester Cantor's house, though." My voice caught. "He's dead."

She gasped. "Oh, my gosh, Marcy! I'm so sorry. You don't think it had anything to do with that treasure map business, do you?"

"Yeah, I do." I placed my pattern and the book with the photo I was using as a reference onto the ottoman. Then I stood and wiped my hands down the sides of my jeans. "I'll be back in a couple minutes. This shouldn't take long."

"Are you sure?" she asked. "I mean, do you know for certain that it's Ted you want, or were you just upset over the news about Mr. Cantor? If that's it, Todd will forgive you for kissing Ted, and—"

"I'm sure." And I was. Looking back, I'd always been more attracted to Ted than to Todd, but I'd been reluctant to hurt Todd's feelings, not to mention Sadie's and Blake's feelings. Todd and I were friends— good friends—and I didn't want to blow that. I hoped my decision wouldn't destroy that friendship. But I had to follow my heart. My heart chose Ted.

The sunshine was still favoring Tallulah Falls with its presence when I stepped out onto the sidewalk, and it felt heavenly. The drab rainy days had left me aching for the warmth and sunshine I'd enjoyed in San Francisco during the early spring each year. I stepped over to the crosswalk, waited for the signal, and walked over to the Brew Crew.

The craft pub brewery wasn't very crowded this time of day—it was just past noon—and Todd spotted me the moment I walked in. He was polishing the bar with a white cloth. I raised a hand in greeting and he jerked his head upward in something of a reverse nod. He wasn't glad to see me—that was obvious.

I took a deep breath and strode to the bar. "Got a second?"

He surveyed the pub, taking note of two waitresses cleaning tables and his other bartender Robbie taking inventory. "Come on into the office."

I followed him into his office, where he closed the door behind us.

"So . . ." He spread his hands. "I guess you and Ted are getting along better than I'd thought."

"He'd stopped by to tell me that Chester Cantor was found murdered in his home," I said.

"I'm sorry to hear that." He stepped forward and put his hands on my shoulders. I could tell he wanted to hug me but was hesitant. "That's what was going on in your office? Nash was consoling you . . . and that led to the kiss?"

"That's a big part of it, but I want to give the relationship a chance," I said softly. "I'm sorry you found out the way you did."

He dropped his hands from my shoulders and shrugged. "It's no big deal. I was just coming over to apologize for Keira and the treasure map episode. Sadie had told me about it, and I knew Keira did it because of me."

"Yeah." I grinned slightly. "That girl has it bad for you."

"Only she's not the one I want." He ran his hand through his hair.

I placed my hand on his arm. "I'm sorry, Todd. I think the world of you. I really do. I just . . ."

He nodded. "I got it. You like me, but you like Marshal Dillon better. It's not rocket science."

"You'll—"

He held up his hand to stop me from continuing. "Save the platitudes, all right? Yes, we can still be friends. Yes, there's someone out there for me, and I'll meet the right girl, *yadda*, *yadda*. But I'm not ready to move on to all that yet. Just give me some space, okay?"

I nodded, tears burning my eyes. Not trusting myself to speak, I turned and left.

"How'd he take it?" Sadie asked with an edge to her voice as soon as I walked back into the Seven-Year Stitch. She was standing with her back against the counter and her arms folded.

I slid my hands into the front pockets of my jeans. "He's a little upset." I lifted and dropped one shoulder. What did she expect me to say?

"Probably more than a little," she said. "I should go over and check on him."

"Please, don't make a bigger deal out of this than it is. Todd asked me to give him some space. I think he'd appreciate that from you and Blake as well."

"Yeah? Well, maybe he'd like to know his friends care about him."

I shook my head. "Can't you be happy for me in the least?"

Sadie blew out a breath and dropped her arms to her sides. After a moment she said, "I am happy for you . . . and for Ted, too, for that matter. I'm just sorry for Todd. And I blame myself for trying to throw the two of you together. I wish you and Todd had been able to give your relationship a fair shake."

"I think we were able to do that," I said. "But my feelings for Ted go beyond friendship. My feelings for Todd don't. Maybe Keira is the girl for him after all."

"I don't think so." Sadie looked down at the floor. "There was never anything between her and Todd except on her part . . . kinda like the opposite of you and Todd, right?"

"That's not fair. I can't help who I have feelings for."

"I know," Sadie said, with a huff. "I'm sorry."

"You know who you should introduce Todd to? Audrey Dalton. She's beautiful, and she seems like a terrific person."

Sadie looked up, and I could see that her eyes were glistening with unshed tears. "Yeah . . . but, after this, Todd might never trust anyone with his heart again."

I thought Sadie was being a tad melodramatic, but I had the good sense not to say so.

After Sadie left, I gave Angus a treat and made myself a cup of tea. She hadn't made me feel any better about how things had gone with Todd. But, fortunately, she hadn't made me feel any worse. As I'd told her, I couldn't help it that I had feelings for Ted. I thought about Ted and smiled to myself. He was a wonderful man. If I had a future with any guy in Tallulah Falls, it was Ted.

I sat down at the computer and pulled up the photos I'd taken of Mr. Cantor's tapestry. This brought on another wave of melancholy over Mr. Cantor's tragic death. This was one of the most bittersweet days I'd ever experienced. I'd have to call Mom later and get her take on everything.

I tried to put Mr. Cantor's death out of my mind and concentrate solely on the tapestry. *The Delia*. I could quickly see if it was a legitimate shipwreck.

I went into my Internet browser and did a search for shipwrecks off the coast of Tallulah Falls, Oregon. The *Delia* came up in the search. I clicked the link.

The Delia *was an East Coast ship that sank off the coast of Tallulah Falls en route to Portland, Oregon,*

from San Francisco in 1844. The schooner was haul-
ing silk, pearls, and beeswax. The Delia *ran into a*
gale and was stranded at sea. A tugboat arrived too
late to rescue the stranded vessel, but the crew was
taken to safety. The Delia *began to break up in the*
stormy seas, and the cargo was lost.

My cell phone rang, and I took it from my pocket. It was Ted.

"Hi, there," I said.

"You sound as if you're feeling better," he said. "I'm glad. I know it was rough on you to hear about Mr. Cantor's death."

"It was. Did your investigators find the names of any treasure hunters when they were searching the home? Mr. Cantor said he'd spoken with one."

"And you think that might be a good place to start, eh, Inch-High Private Eye?"

I laughed softly at the twisted endearment. "It couldn't hurt."

"I'll look into it. In the meantime, you shouldn't worry about the investigation," he said.

"And you shouldn't waste your breath. You know I'm going to worry about Mary and Melanie as long as they're in that house. What if Adam is the killer?"

"Can we discuss it over dinner? At my place? I'll make my famous chicken piccata."

"Well, if it's *famous*, how could I say no?" I asked.

"Oh, it's famous, all right. How about I pick you up at your place at six?"

"That sounds great. I'm looking forward to it."

I heard a customer come into the shop and had to hang up. But as soon as this customer left, I was calling Mom.

"Hi. Welcome to the Seven-Year Stitch," I told the woman as I replaced my phone in my jeans pocket. The woman with the lank brown hair pulled into a low ponytail looked vaguely familiar, but I couldn't place her right away. Had she visited the shop before?

She looked around appreciatively. "This is a nice place." She nodded toward Angus, who seemed to sense her hesitation. "He doesn't bite, does he?"

"No. Angus is as friendly as can be."

"It's real nice of you to help Ms. Singh out and all," she said, still avoiding Angus as if she wasn't a hundred percent sure she could trust him.

That's when it clicked. She was one of the women in the domestic abuse victims group. Melanie Cantor had sat between this woman and her mother yesterday evening. "I'm glad I'm able to contribute, even if it is in such a small way."

Susan . . . I was fairly certain her name was Susan.

"Oh, I don't think it's a small way at all." She moved farther into the shop and smiled at the mannequin standing behind the counter. "Cute. Hey, did you guys talk with Mary's father-in-law this morning? I know that was weighing on Mary's mind awfully heavy last night."

I wasn't sure what to say. I didn't want to be the one to tell Mary's friend that Mr. Cantor was dead. Who knows what kind of rumors and speculation that would start? So I simply said, "We did. He's a real sweetheart." To change the subject, I added, "Is there anything I can help you find?"

"No, I'm just browsing," she said. "Thanks, though." She wandered over to the pattern books. "I appreciate your bringing us the stamped pattern kits. These with the symbols look hard."

"They're not so bad when you get the hang of it," I assured her. "You might want to try one after you finish the project you're working on now."

"Maybe."

As she continued to thumb through the pattern books, another customer came in asking if I had anything on Chinese Suzhou embroidery. The young woman was of Asian-American descent and told me she was trying to combine her Chinese heritage with her love of needlework.

Suzhou embroidery is one of the oldest embroidery techniques in the world and utilizes brightly colored silk threads to create intricately detailed needlework pieces. I mean, *really intricate*. One form of Suzhou embroidery even features a design—either the same design or a different one—on the back of the fabric. Can you imagine? And, no, I've never done one of these myself. I was doing well to create the image on the front of the fabric.

It has been recorded that Suzhou embroidery was being done as far back as 200 BC, but the technique became popular during the Song Dynasty (which began in the late 900s, if I'm not mistaken). I was impressed that one of my customers was interested in the craft.

Although I didn't have anything in stock, I retrieved my laptop from my office and invited the customer to help me find something among my suppliers. She and I sat on one of the sofas in the sit-and-stitch square and scrolled through Web pages until we found a supplier who offered Suzhou kits. She and I were both thrilled, and I ordered four kits—one for her, and three to put in the shop. The customer gave me her name, e-mail address, and cell number, and I promised to let her know as soon as the kits came in.

Once the Suzhou customer had left, I turned my attention back to Susan, but she'd apparently slipped out of the shop. I checked the clock and saw that it was a quarter past three. Since there's usually a lull in business at that time of day, I decided to call Mom. As a sought-after costume designer, she was often away on location. But she was enjoying some much deserved downtime at home this week.

She answered on the first ring, and instead of

chirping her lyrical *Beverly Singer*, she answered with, "Hello, darling. What's new?"

"You actually checked caller ID!" I laughed. "*That's* new."

She joined in my laughter. "Hey, I'm on vacation . . . or, rather, staycation. I'm being careful about whose calls I take. Now, let me guess why you're calling." She paused. "You found another dead body in your storeroom."

"Mom! Of course not!"

"You mean there *hasn't* been a murder in Tallulah Falls lately?"

I hesitated just an instant too long.

"Marcella," she said, forcing a note of sternness into her voice. "Tell me what's going on."

I quickly explained about teaching embroidery to the domestic abuse victims group, speaking with Mary and Melanie, and Mr. Cantor's demise.

"I'm so sorry, darling," she said. "What about the woman and her daughter? Did they still leave?"

"No. Mary couldn't bear the thought of leaving Adam when he would be grieving for the loss of his father."

"That makes sense. She loves the man . . . just not his treatment of her," Mom said.

"Yeah. . . . I didn't intend to call you with such depressing news. I wanted to tell you about Ted . . . and me."

She chuckled softly. "It's about time you saw what was right in front of you. Well, I'm happy for you."

"Thank you." What she'd said prior to being happy for me slowly dawned on me. "Wait. It's about time? What's that supposed to mean?"

"Oh, love, I could tell when I was there the last time that the good detective was completely smitten with you and that the feeling was mutual."

"Why didn't you say anything?" I asked.

"It wasn't for me to say. I knew your heart would lead you in the right direction."

I huffed, a little put out at how well she knew me and my heart. "What if I'd called and told you I was in a relationship with Todd?"

"But you didn't," she said simply. "Granted, if you had, I'd have been surprised . . . and worried. There's no chemistry between you and Todd. And, believe me, I know chemistry when I see it."

"You could tell that Todd and I don't have feelings for each other but that Ted and I do?" I asked.

"Of course, darling. I mean, it's obvious that you *care* about Todd, and he's certainly infatuated with you. But you and Ted share something more passionate . . . more lasting," she said. "Does Todd know?"

"Um . . . yeah. He walked in on Ted and me kissing in my office."

"Ooh. So he got a jarring revelation rather than a

gentle letdown. That's not ideal. Have you seen him since then?"

"I had Sadie come and watch the shop while I went over to the Brew Crew," I said. "He didn't want to talk with me about it."

"Ah, darling, you can hardly blame him there. Bruised ego, ruffled feathers . . . all that jazz. How did Sadie take the news?"

"Not well. She blames herself for Todd's broken heart."

Mom scoffed. "Todd did not get his heart broken. As I said, he was infatuated, but he was not in love with you. If he had been, he wouldn't have dragged his feet about asking you to that masquerade ball back in February."

"Hey, that's right."

"Of course, I'm right. I'm always right. I'm your mother. Plus, I work in Hollywood. I can always tell true emotions from shallow attractions . . . no matter how real others—even some of the ones with the feelings—believe them to be."

I laughed, relieved because I knew Mom was right. "Oh, Mom, I love you."

"I know," she said, laughter evident in her voice. "And I love you."

"I know," I replied. "You're not the only one with insights and inside information."

Chapter Six

After talking with Mom, I logged on to my computer and did an Internet search for professional treasure hunters on the Pacific coast. There weren't any Web sites I could find for individual treasure hunters, but I did find a professional association page. I clicked through to the discussion forum and read enough to learn that while some of the treasure seekers limited their efforts to trolling beaches with metal detectors, some were actually in the business of finding and salvaging ships. I registered as a guest and asked if anyone on the forum had ever spoken with Chester Cantor about helping him with a project off the coast of Tallulah Falls, Oregon. I left my e-mail address—marcys@7yrstitch—for interested respondents to contact me. The fact remained that the Cantor family had financial problems and that Chester had died wanting to alleviate

them. I'd promised to help him. I intended to keep
my promise.

After I'd finished trolling the Internet for treasure
hunters, I looked for a way to facilitate the Fabergé
egg project. I didn't have much luck and decided this
might take some creative thinking on my part. Unfortunately, I didn't have much time to invest in it today
since it was half past four. I dusted the furniture in
between waiting on customers while that half hour
crawled by.

Finally, it was five o'clock, the moment I'd been
anxiously waiting for all day. I hustled Angus into
the Jeep, and we headed home to get ready for my
date with Ted . . . my *first* date with Ted in a sense. I
mean, I realized I'd been out with Ted before, but
our relationship had taken a turn—a whirl? a spin?—
this morning. So, in a way, this date really was a first.
It was special.

I wondered what to wear. We were having dinner
at his house, so I didn't want to dress formally. But I
didn't want to dress too casually either.

I giggled. "I've got a boyfriend, Angus!"

From the backseat, he woofed his approval before
slurping my ear with his tongue.

We were at a stoplight, so I briefly hugged his face
to mine with one hand while keeping the other
firmly on the steering wheel. "You know you're still
the head honcho around here, though."

He opened his mouth in what appeared to be a wide grin before the light turned and I had to focus my attention on the road again.

When I got home, I fed Angus and then hurried upstairs to turn on the water in the bathtub. The entire time the tub was filling, I was standing in front of my closet. I must've pulled out and returned every article of clothing in it at least twice. I finally decided on black trousers, a gray silk blouse, and strappy silver sandals. I was grateful I'd given myself a pedicure midway through the week.

After choosing my outfit, I rushed to the bathroom and had to drain a couple of inches of water from the tub so it wouldn't overflow when I got in. How great would that have been for Ted to come and catch me soaked, disheveled, and frantically running the wet vac?

I took a deep breath, sank into the tub, and used my favorite scented bath gel. It was wonderfully floral and romantic, and it calmed my jagged nerves.

It was ridiculous to be so nervous about this date with Ted . . . and, yet, I was. I wanted everything to be perfect. I wanted to be certain I'd made the right choice.

Ted arrived at about a quarter to six. I was putting my jet chandelier earrings in as I walked down the steps to open the door. He looked fantastic: dark jeans, a navy pinstripe dress shirt, a brown leather jacket.

He handed me a single red rose. "Pretty corny, huh?"

I smiled. "Pretty sweet." Despite the heels, I had to put my hand on the back of his neck to draw him down for a kiss. "Let me put this rosebud in water and let Angus into the house, and then we can go."

"I have to admit I'm kinda nervous," he called to me from the foyer. "Doesn't that sound crazy?"

I grinned to myself and wondered if I should tell him I was feeling a little nervous too. *Naaah.* Instead I let Angus in through the back door, and he raced through the kitchen to see Ted.

"Hey, buddy," Ted said, stooping down to energetically pet Angus with both hands.

"He used to make you nervous too," I reminded Ted.

He laughed. "Yeah, he did, didn't he?"

"So, you're making your *famous* chicken piccata for me, huh?"

"Yep. Speaking of which, we'd better be going." On the drive to his apartment, he confessed that it wasn't necessarily his *famous* chicken piccata but it was actually an easy go-to dish his mother had taught him before he left home for college.

Ted's apartment complex consisted of three identical chocolate-and-tan two-story buildings, each sectioned into four individual units. Signs in front of the buildings designated their names: the Westchester, the Somerville, and the Lincoln. Ted's apartment was the end unit on the right side of the Westchester.

The apartments' landscaping was beautiful. Small evergreen trees, smooth white rocks, and round beige stepping-stones lined the walkways from the parking lots to the apartments and the common areas. Each building had two covered maple swings— one at either end. With the verandas on the back of each unit, residents were assured of plenty of room to enjoy the outdoors.

"Welcome to my humble, messy home," Ted said, opening the door to the apartment.

I stepped inside and looked around. "You call *this* messy?"

The living room looked more like a just-passing-through room. There was no clutter, no dust, and certainly no mess. The walls were painted taupe, and much of the room was taken up by a long black leather sofa. Directly across from the sofa was a beige brick fireplace. The stone reminded me of those outside, and I appreciated the designer's attention to the cohesive aesthetic.

Above the fireplace was a flat-screen television. Its remote control was on the coffee table in front of the sofa. The only other thing on the table was a tray of cork-backed coasters with the Tallulah Falls light-house on the front. To the right of the sofa was a matching chair with a neatly folded red-and-black-plaid blanket lying on the seat. A silver floor lamp gleamed in the corner.

Built-in shelves on either side of the fireplace held a Blu-ray disc player, a video game console and con-trollers, and an assortment of video games. There was also an eclectic mix of books on the shelves: the Holy Bible, books on forensics and biometrics, crim-inology textbooks, a volume of Keats poetry, and popular fiction by Koontz, Coben, and Deaver. You can tell a lot about a man by the books he reads. Ted was a complex man—even more so than I'd origi-nally realized.

I smiled up at him. "I love your apartment. It's very Ted Nash."

He dropped a quick kiss on my lips. "Thank you . . . I think. I just hope that after you've seen the whole place, you won't be disappointed."

"I won't be."

"Ah, but you haven't seen my office yet," he said. "It's where I go to think. But it can wait until after we eat. I'm starving." He took my hand and led me to the kitchen.

Like the living room, the kitchen was neat, tidy, and efficient. The appliances were stainless steel, the cabinets were glossy black with thin, tubular silver

handles, and the countertops were dark gray gran-
ite. The room would have appeared too dark had it
not been for the skylights and recessed lighting over
the island and the chandelier over the table in the
breakfast nook. I noticed with pleasure that Ted had
set the table—complete with two white taper candles in the center—and had white wine chilling.

"You've thought of everything," I told him.

"I wanted tonight to be special."

"It is," I said.

He smiled and—did I detect the hint of a blush?—
went to the sink and washed his hands.

"Can I help?" I asked.

"Sure." He dried his hands on a kitchen towel on
a hook by the sink. "You can sit here and talk to me
while I cook for you."

I sat down on one of the high-backed stools in
front of the island. "Have you lived here long?"

"A couple years . . . I moved here when Jen and I
split up."

"That must've been hard," I said.

"Divorce is never easy. One of my friends—an
older guy who'd been both divorced and widowed—
said death was easier to go through. He said he
didn't have the lingering questions or doubts and
that he didn't feel as if his time had been wasted."

I tilted my head toward my shoulder. "Not sure I
agree with that last part. Love given is never really

wasted, is it? I mean, I've been hurt in the past, but I have to believe that putting my heart out there and being willing to take a chance made me grow into the person I am today."

He gave me a warm, lazy smile. "I'm glad you're taking a chance on me."

"You're worth the gamble."

"So are you," Ted said. He took my face in his hands and gave me a slow, thorough kiss.

"I'm glad you're taking a chance on me too," I said.

"Hmm . . . let's see. . . . You're beautiful, loving, smart, independent . . . heck, the girl of my dreams. Why *wouldn't* I take a chance on you?" He laughed. "I'd better get my mind back on our dinner."

"I'll change the subject then. How did Adam Cantor take the news of his father's death?" I asked.

"Wow. I wasn't ready for a topic *that* serious yet. Pour us a glass of wine, would you?"

I did as he asked, handed him a glass of wine, put mine on the island, and sat back down. Ted took the chicken breasts, which he'd already butterflied, from the refrigerator and placed them in flour on a small plate. He salted and peppered them before dredging them through the flour and placing them into a frying pan with olive oil and butter.

Finally, he turned to me. "Adam didn't take it

well. He seemed legitimately shocked and devastated."

"So you aren't considering him a suspect?"

"I didn't say that." He frowned. "I've been on the force long enough to know that people can fool you, but I didn't get the feeling he was faking his grief."

"What about Melanie?" I asked. "She must be heartbroken."

Ted nodded. "And I think she's kind of scared."

"Was she told that her grandfather was murdered?"

He used a fork to gently turn the chicken breasts. "No. But she knows that now they aren't leaving, and I think that's why she's scared. Officer Dayton talked with her and her mother in the school guidance counselor's office before Mary took Melanie home. Melanie wanted to know how mad her dad was and if anyone had let their plans slip to him."

"Poor kid."

He sighed. "It's sad. She loves Adam—she and Mary both do—but they can't live with his violent temper."

"Why won't he get help?"

"Because he doesn't think he has a problem," Ted said.

"Do you have any other suspects in the murder?"

He grinned at me over his shoulder. "We're working on it, Inch-High. We're working on it."

We finished the main course, and then Ted took a turtle cheesecake from the refrigerator.

"That looks terrific," I said. "Did you make that too?"

"Of course." He grinned. "I made it down to the bakery and picked it up."

I laughed. "I'm really stuffed right now. Can we save it for later? I want to see the rest of your apartment."

"You want to see my mess, huh?"

"I do."

Shaking his head, he returned the cheesecake to the fridge. "Follow me."

I pushed back my chair, stood, and joined Ted in the hallway.

He gestured to the right. "As you can see, this room is the bedroom."

Like the living room and kitchen, the walls were painted dark taupe. This room had white molding, which provided a stark and interesting contrast. In the middle of the far wall was a king-sized mahogany sleigh bed.

An overstuffed navy recliner was in the corner. By the recliner was a magazine rack filled with detective, crime, and sports magazines and a remote control. A small television was mounted on the opposite wall. On the wall above the bed, a photo collage of the Oregon coast at sunset was displayed.

There were matching nightstands on either side of the bed, and I noticed that the one on the right obviously got the most use. "You sleep on the right side," I mused.

"Yeah. Is that okay?"

"Sure." I could feel my face burning. "Um . . . let's see that nightmare of an office."

The office was, indeed, on the messy side—especially when compared to the rest of the apartment. Like the kitchen, the office carried over the black-and-silver color scheme. A black desk and manager's chair sat in the middle of the room. There was a laptop on the desk, but I couldn't see much of what else was on the desk for the loose papers and file folders scattered on top of it. Against one wall were three tall silver filing cabinets.

On the longest wall was a white dry-erase board. One side of the board contained writing that had been partially erased. The other side had been wiped clean, and CHESTER CANTOR had been written at the top. Beneath Mr. Cantor's name, there were two columns titled SUSPECTS and MOTIVATION. In the *Suspects* column, Ted had written ADAM CANTOR. Under Adam's name was written TREASURE HUNTER, and under that was UNSUB. There was nothing written in the motivation column.

"What's an UNSUB?" I asked.

"Unknown subject," Ted answered. "This case is going to be tough. The old guy didn't really go anywhere, so it's hard to imagine he had any enemies."

"Other than the one under his own roof."

"There *is* that. But, as I told you earlier, Adam seemed honestly hurt by his father's death." He sighed. "I'm still waiting, though, to see if his alibi checks out." He gently turned me toward the door. "Let's try not to think about Chester's death anymore tonight."

"Sounds good to me." I didn't know if that was entirely possible, though—for Ted or for me.

He took my hand and led me out onto the veranda. He had a tan wicker glider and two chairs facing the mountains. In the corner was a large gas grill, which was currently covered. A small glass-topped table sat between the two chairs.

Ted and I sat on the glider, and he slipped his arm around my shoulder. As I nestled against his side, listened to the distant surf, and gazed up at the stars, I knew I'd made not just the right choice but the *only* choice.

Chapter Seven

When Angus and I got to the shop the next morning, the first thing I did was check my e-mail. Sure enough, one of the treasure hunters from the discussion forum had e-mailed me. He said he'd like to meet and that he'd stop by my shop "tomorrow morning."

I checked the date of the e-mail and saw that he'd sent it last night. Then I racked my brain to determine if I'd given any information about myself in the message I'd posted on the forum. I'd hoped to be at least a little ambiguous about my identity in case Chester Cantor's murderer read the forum entries.

I was thinking maybe I should call Ted and tell him what was going on when the bells over the door jangled to let me know I had a customer. Or, at least, I *hoped* it was a customer.

I stepped out of my office to see that Angus had

already greeted the rather grizzled-looking older gentleman who'd entered the shop.

"He's a beaut, he is!" the man exclaimed, scratching Angus on the head.

"Thank you," I said. I'd already guessed who the man was, but I decided to play dumb. "How may I help you?"

"Well, I saw your message on the treasure hunters' Web site, and I'd talked with Chester about helping him find the treasure from the *Delia*."

He had the name of the ship correct. He must've really spoken with Mr. Cantor. "How'd you find me?"

"From your e-mail. I'd heard of the Seven-Year Stitch—the name always struck me as funny—so when I saw it was part of your address, I figured you worked here."

"You figured right," I said, with a small smile. "Would you like to have a seat?"

"Sure. You got any coffee?" he asked.

"I do, but I haven't had a chance to get it started yet this morning. I'll do that."

"I'd appreciate it," he said. "A fresh-brewed cup of joe sounds awfully nice."

I went into the office and prepared the coffeepot. The man seemed friendly and harmless enough. He obviously hadn't given Angus any reason not to like him, and dogs sense things like . . . murderous intent . . . right? And the treasure hunter appeared to be old enough to be one of Mr. Cantor's contemporaries. Maybe he was legitimate and wouldn't kill me for the tapestry . . . which I no longer even had.

"The coffee should be ready in about five minutes," I said, returning to the sit-and-stitch square. "So had Mr. Cantor hired you to help him find a treasure?"

"Not yet. No money had exchanged hands. My son has a boat—gives some dolphin tours and stuff like that—and he'd love to get into the salvage business," the man said. "I'm Jack Powell, by the way." He stretched an arm across the coffee table so I could shake his hand.

"Nice to meet you, Mr. Powell. I'm Marcy Singer."

"Good to know you, Marcy. Call me Jack."

I smiled. "Jack."

"Anyway, back to Chester. He and I and my boy were trying to come up with a way to get the money we'd need to start the search. None of the three of us had much savings or seed money or whatever to go on, and we knew we'd need depth recorders, diving equipment, and underwater metal detectors. I guess we can forget about it though now that Chester's dead."

"Did Mr. Cantor ever show you the map?" I asked.

Jack shook his head. "Nope. Chester was kinda

paranoid about that map. I reckon he thought that if anyone else saw it, they'd cut him out of the loop."

"I guess I can understand that. He showed me the tapestry that he believed contained the map," I said. "But I think his belief that it was a treasure map was only wishful thinking."

"I wouldn't be so sure about that, Marcy. There are enough legends and reports of treasure found off the Pacific coast that if we could've scraped the money together, we'd have looked for it."

I excused myself and went and got our coffee. I put the coffee and a handful of creamers and sweeteners on a tray and returned to the sit-and-stitch square. I placed the tray on the coffee table before handing Jack a cup of coffee.

Jack loaded up his cup with sugar, stirred the steaming beverage briefly, and then took a loud slurp. "A man could have riches to pass down through three generations—at least—if he could find just one of the treasures reputed to be somewhere on this coast."

"But those are just legends, aren't they?" I asked. "Has anyone ever found anything of real substance near Tallulah Falls?"

"You can go right over to the Columbia River Maritime Museum in Astoria and see a chunk of beeswax and a block of wood recovered from a seventeenth-century Manila galleon shipwreck," he said. "Astoria isn't all *that* far from here. The museum has got some fur trader tokens too."

"But those items wouldn't make a person rich, would they?" I asked. "Besides, wouldn't you think everything that had been lost would have already been found by now?"

"Not necessarily. In June of 2011, divers off the Florida Keys found an antique emerald ring worth about half a million dollars—along with several other artifacts—thought to be from the *Nuestra Señora de Atocha*. It was one of the most famous Spanish ships of its day, and it sank in 1622." Jack took another drink of his coffee. "Most of the wreckage was recovered in 1985, but there was still enough hanging around to give someone else a payday. I think the same might be true of the *Delia* . . . although no one that I know of has ever reported finding any of its treasure."

I made a mental note to check out the *Nuestra Señora de Atocha* on the Internet to validate the veracity of Jack's information. "So there really could be something out there—something that somebody might kill Chester Cantor to get their hands on."

Jack raised his brows. "Now, don't go thinking I did Chester in! My son and I needed Chester and his map to help us know where to begin."

"Oh, I know. I didn't mean that at all," I said. "I was just thinking out loud. Did you know Chester very well?"

"I'd say I knew him fairly well. Why?"

"Do you know of anyone who'd want to hurt him?"

"Only that boy of his. One time Chester had this bruise on his left cheek." Jack shook his head. "Man, it was nasty looking. I asked him what happened, and he said Adam had hit him. My boy wanted to have it out with Adam over it, but Chester asked him not to. He said that Adam hadn't meant to do it and that confronting him about it would only make things worse."

"I'm sorry to hear that. I just met him briefly, but Mr. Cantor seemed like a terrific person."

"Yeah, Chester was a real stand-up guy." He took one last drink of his coffee. "You don't happen to remember what the map looked like, do you?"

"I'm afraid not." I was telling the truth. I *didn't* remember what the map looked like. He didn't ask if I had photographs of the tapestry. I wasn't ready to tip my hand to Jack Powell just yet. I wasn't entirely sure I trusted him.

After Jack Powell left, I called Ted. My call went to voice mail, so I thanked him for last night's dinner and asked him to give me a call about a treasure hunter I'd spoken with earlier this morning.

I then decided to start from scratch on the Fabergé

egg project. When I'd first hatched this idea (pun intended!), I'd had no clue that it would be so difficult. I took the photograph I'd printed out and carefully traced the outline of the egg and its design. I uploaded my black-and-white image onto my computer and once again imported it into my cross-stitch software. Using the photo as a guide, I used the program's library of thread colors to re-create the image. I was really pleased with the end result and printed out my new and improved pattern.

I was walking out of the office when Ted came into the shop.

I smiled. "Hi, there."

"Hi." He held up his phone. "I was in a meeting with Manu when you called. What's this about your conversation with a treasure hunter?"

We went over to the navy sofa facing the window and sat down. Angus followed and placed his head on Ted's knee. It was spring and Angus was shedding, so I was glad for Ted's sake that he was wearing jeans and a dress shirt today rather than a suit. The jeans would be easier to brush off.

"Yesterday I got on a local treasure hunter discussion forum and asked if anyone had talked with Chester Cantor about helping him find a treasure off the coast of Tallulah Falls," I said. "This morning, my sole respondent showed up to talk over his previous plans with Mr. Cantor."

Ted rubbed his forehead. "You asked him to meet you here?"

"No, of course not. He found me through my e-mail address. Who knew some random old sailor would be familiar with the name of an embroidery shop?" I went on to recount my conversation with Jack Powell. "My gut says he's not our guy, but I think you should talk with him and determine whether or not he has an alibi for the time of the murder."

He shook his head and gave me a bemused grin. "I'll do that. Do you mind if I take the case back over now, Inch-High?"

"Not at all, Detective. I have an egg to stitch." I held up my pattern.

"We could simply color eggs the old-fashioned way," he said. "It'd be quicker."

"Oh, we'll do that," I promised. "But I'm sending this one to Mom."

"Speaking of Mom . . ." He let the sentence hang.

"She approves wholeheartedly."

He laughed. "I'm glad. Want to have dinner at Captain Moe's tonight?"

"I'd love it."

He stood. "I'd better go see if Jack Powell has an alibi for yesterday afternoon."

"Wait a sec." I hopped up from the sofa and retrieved the lint roller from beneath the counter. "Let me roll you before you go."

He chuckled. "That is such a loaded statement . . . but I'm not saying a word."

"Thank you." I quickly ran the lint roller over his clothing and gave him a peck on the lips. "I'll see you later."

After Ted left, my thoughts drifted to the Cantor family. I decided to take them a muffin basket and express my sympathy for their loss. Plus, ordering the basket from MacKenzies' Mochas would allow me to test the water with Blake and Sadie too.

Before I could call MacKenzies' Mochas, I had a string of customers and a package delivery. I rang up the last of the customers and decided to hurriedly make the call before the next wave rolled through. Saturdays were usually busy—which was a good thing . . . make that an *excellent* thing—but they didn't give me much time to take care of personal business.

Blake answered the phone.

"Hey," I said. "It's Marcy." I ran my words together, nervous about what he might say to me about Todd or Ted or whatever else might be on his mind. "I'd like to order a muffin basket, please."

"Sure. Will you be picking it up after you close the shop?" he asked.

"Yes, please."

"Is it for the Cantors? Sadie told me about Adam's dad."

"Yeah," I said.

"That's a real tragedy. I'm especially sorry for Melanie." He expelled a breath. "She's particularly fond of our chocolate, chocolate chip muffins, so I'll be sure and include several of those."

"Thanks, Blake." And then I had to ask, "Are you mad at me?"

"Of course not, sweetie. You had to follow your heart, or else you'd end up making yourself and everyone else—including Todd—miserable in the long run."

"Sadie's mad at me," I said.

He chuckled. "She's disappointed, but she'll get over it," he said. "I'll get your basket fixed up, and I'll look forward to seeing you later."

"Thank you."

As we hung up, Vera Langhorne breezed into the shop. Vera was a widow in her early sixties who was one of my first customers and friends here in Tallulah Falls.

"Good morning, dear," she said to me. She stooped down—despite the fact that she was wearing a pink sweater—and hugged Angus. "And how's my sweet boy? Huh? He's such a good boy. Yes, he is!"

Angus was delighted by Vera's gushing over him. His tail, and very nearly his entire body, wagged furiously.

Vera straightened and brushed a lock of her professionally styled and highlighted hair back off her face. She noticed the box sitting on the corner of the counter. "Restocking stuff or new stuff?"

"Something new." I smiled as I cut the tape and carefully opened the box. I took out a thin book and handed it to Vera. I got another out to thumb through myself. "Pincushion patterns. Aren't they adorable?"

"They are! I love them!" She bit her lip as she flipped through the pages. "You know, you should make up some of these and sell them at the counter . . . you know, as impulse items."

"That's not a bad idea."

"I'd buy one . . . or more," she said.

"I could also use the small patterns to make greeting cards," I told her, pleased with my sudden inspiration. I often made greeting cards to have on hand to send to my friends. Why not have them at my customers' disposal as well?

Vera moved over to the sit-and-stitch square with Angus at her heels. "I'd buy several of those. I'd love for people to think that I'd made them hand-stitched cards. They'd think I was such a Martha Stewart." She cocked her head. "There's something different about you today."

I could feel the color rising in my cheeks. I picked up the lint roller and took it over to Vera. "You'll need this when Angus gets through with you," I said as I sat on the red club chair nearest Vera.

"Thanks." She placed the lint roller on the coffee table and continued to scrutinize me. "All right. Who's the lucky fellow?"

"What're you talking about?"

"Don't play coy with me, Marcy Singer. You've got the same look I had when I started dating Paul—happy, excited, eager to see what the future might hold. . . . So?"

Paul Samms was a reporter Vera had met when he interviewed her after our harrowing experience following a masquerade ball a few weeks earlier.

I grinned. "It's Ted."

She clapped her hands together. "I knew it! You two are perfect for each other."

"I'm glad you think so."

"How's Todd taking the news?" she asked. "Or have you told him?"

"He knows," I said. "Of course, he wasn't happy about it . . . and neither was Sadie."

"They'll come around." She patted Angus's head tenderly. "Won't they, boy? Of course, they will."

"Did you know Chester Cantor?" I asked, eager to step out of Vera's glaring spotlight on my love life.

"Yes. I was sorry to hear about his death. The rumor is that Chester didn't die of natural causes."

"No. I . . . um . . . I heard the same rumor," I said.

I didn't feel it was my place to tell Vera what I knew about Mr. Cantor's death. "I only met Mr. Cantor once, but he seemed to be an awfully nice man."

Vera tilted her head. "He'd mellowed in his old age. But, I suppose we all do, hmm?"

"So he wasn't always so kind?"

"Well, he ran off and left his wife and infant son high and dry. There was nothing nice about that," she said.

"I'd heard that he'd divorced Adam's mother," I said. "But I had no idea Adam was an infant when his father left. No wonder he was reluctant to reconcile with Mr. Cantor later on."

"It was a terribly sad situation," Vera said. "Adam's mom, Blanche, worked at the textile mill that was on the outskirts of town back then. Her mother kept the baby while Blanche worked. But she could still barely make ends meet. I believe that's why she wound up marrying that horrible Pete Jenkins."

"Mr. Jenkins was the stepfather who was abusive to Adam?" I asked.

Vera nodded. "And to Blanche too."

"Did Blanche finally leave Mr. Jenkins, or are they still together?"

"Pete died in a logging accident when Adam was fourteen or fifteen," Vera said. "I think that's when Chester started trying to reconnect with Adam."

"Despite the abuse, do you think Adam considered Mr. Jenkins more of a father than Mr. Cantor?" I asked.

"Of course, he did. Pete was the only dad Adam had ever known." She pursed her lips. "I have to hand it to Chester, though. He'd apparently had a true change of heart—at least, where his son was concerned—because he never gave up. It took him two years of letters, cards, and showing up at every sporting event Adam played in . . . and even the ones where Adam sat on the bench . . . before Adam would finally give Chester a chance to be a father to him again."

Chapter Eight

I locked Angus inside the shop while I ran down the street to MacKenzies' Mochas to get the muffin basket for the Cantors. He walked with me as far as the window would allow and then barked his disapproval as I continued on down the street without him. I'd already told him I'd only be a minute. That dog can be so impatient sometimes.

I half wished I could've taken him with me because I was a little nervous about going into the coffee shop. I hadn't spoken with Sadie since yesterday afternoon, so I wasn't sure whether or not she'd give me the cold shoulder . . . even if it *would* be unfair if she did. Still, I was glad to see that Blake was the only one manning the counter when I stepped into the shop. He greeted me with a warm smile, which I gratefully reciprocated.

"Hi," I said. "Is the muffin basket ready?"

"It sure is. Let me grab it for you." Blake turned and went to the shelf on the wall behind the counter to retrieve my basket. He'd done a beautiful job on it—purple and white ribbons cascaded from a dual bow—and I complimented his work.

Before he could reply or get back to the counter, Keira sauntered up. She anchored one hand to her hip and looked at me disdainfully. "What're *you* doing here?"

I smiled. "Thanks awfully for your hospitality, Keira, but Blake is already waiting on me."

She huffed and stalked over to the espresso machine.

As Blake put the basket on the counter in front of me and went back to quietly redress Keira for her rudeness, Todd came in. This visit just kept getting better and better. Was he going to glare at me like Keira had done?

"Hi, Marcy," Todd said. He nodded toward the counter. "Blake. Good to see you."

Keira whirled toward Todd, nearly spilling the espresso she'd been pouring. "Hey, babe. Be right with you."

"Keira, I'm serious," Blake said. "I'm not taking much more of your attitude. Now, step it up. Table four is getting impatient."

"You look beautiful," Todd told me as Keira

stormed off with Table Four's espresso. "More so than I've ever seen you."

I looked down at my jeans and pale peach sweat-shirt. "Wow. I should get this dressed up every day."

"It's not the clothes." He took my elbow and gently propelled me into the alcove where the coat hooks were loaded with lightweight jackets and an um-brella or two. "You look happy." He smiled ruefully. "I'm sorry I wasn't the one able to put that sparkle in your eyes. But I'm glad someone was."

"Todd, I never meant—" My voice caught, and my vision was blurred by unshed tears.

He pulled me to him and kissed the top of my head. "Please, don't cry. I just want you to know I realize what we do have, you and I. We have a pow-erful friendship that I don't want to lose."

My *"You won't"* was muffled against his shoulder.

He held me at arm's length then and told me, "If Ted hurts you, he'll have me to contend with."

I smiled. "I know."

"I really care about you, Marcy."

"And I really care about you, Todd. It's just . . ."

"Don't say it. I know." He grinned. "I'd better let you go."

I nodded. I returned to the counter, but Blake had made himself scarce. Beside the muffin basket, he'd left a napkin on which he'd written, *It's on your tab. Love, B.*

As I left, I noticed Todd had already gone too.

When Angus and I got home, I quickly showered and changed into a brown suede skirt, a tan cowl-neck sweater, and knee-high chocolate boots. I'd just finished putting the finishing touches on my hair and makeup when Ted arrived.

I hurried down the stairs, opened the door, and greeted him with a kiss.

"What did I do to deserve that?" he asked.

"Actually, it's what I hope you'll do." I took his hand and led him into the kitchen. With a nod toward the muffin basket sitting on the table, I asked, "Would you mind if we drop this off at the Cantors' house on the way to Captain Moe's?"

"Of course I don't mind." He took a closer look at the basket. "It's from MacKenzies' Mochas?"

I nodded and then busied myself putting food in Angus's dish.

"How did that go?"

"It went fine. Blake was super, and I'm so relieved about that. I didn't see Sadie. Keira was her usual snotty self." I glanced at Ted surreptitiously. "And Todd was . . . gracious."

"Todd?"

"Uh-huh. He came in and told me, basically, that he's happy for me . . . for us." I turned to face Ted. "We hugged it out, and I think we're in a good place now."

"Oh, you hugged it out, huh?" He stepped closer and pulled me into his arms. "Should I be jealous?" He lowered his head and gave me a toe-curling kiss.

"Yes," I answered breathlessly. "If jealousy makes you kiss me like that, then you should stay that way."

"Then consider me your personal green-eyed monster." He kissed me again.

"If you keep that up, we're never going to make it to Captain Moe's," I said.

"Okay, okay," he said, with a laugh. "Are you ready to go?"

"Yep." I got the muffin basket. "Lead the way."

As he opened the car door for me, and I slid onto the seat, I asked, "Is Audrey Dalton seeing anyone?"

Ted frowned. "I have no idea. Why?"

"I think she and Todd would make a good couple."

He shook his head and closed the door. When he got into the car, he asked, "Do you honestly think matchmaking is such a swell idea?"

I shrugged. "Manu and Reggie probably think it is."

"But Sadie and Blake—not so much," said Ted.

*   *   *

There were several cars in front of the Cantor house when Ted and I arrived. Given Adam's reputation, I was surprised so many people were on hand to offer their condolences; but I supposed some were there for Mary and Melanie.

When we walked in, Mary's friend Susan—the one who was in the domestic abuse victims' class and who'd been into the shop yesterday—was sitting beside Mary on the sofa.

Susan rose and took the muffin basket from me. "Thank you, Marcy. I'll put these with the other gifts and cards."

"Thank you," I said. "I'm sorry I didn't get to say good-bye to you before you left the Seven-Year Stitch yesterday."

"That's all right," she said. "I'll stop in again sometime soon."

As Susan took the basket in the direction of the kitchen, I sat down beside Mary. "How are you?"

"I think we're all still kinda in shock." She shook her head slowly. "It's just so hard to believe."

Ted stooped down beside me and spoke softly to Mary. "I want you to know the Tallulah Falls Police Department is doing everything possible."

"Thank you."

Adam chose that particular moment to stagger

over to the sofa. Even three feet away from the guy, I could smell the alcohol on his breath.

"Police are doing everything, huh?" Adam asked, his words slurring. "Everything to find the killer or everything to frame me? Heard you people asked around at work . . . wanted to make sure I was where I said I was. You think I murdered my own father?"

Unfortunately, Melanie was going from her room to the kitchen and overheard Adam's last question. She came into the living room, her small face pinched with sorrow and confusion, her mouth agape.

She looked from her father to her mother. "Is that true? W-was Grandpa . . . ? Did somebody kill him?"

Mary rose and went to hug her daughter.

"Mom, is it true?" Melanie asked, pushing away.

Mary nodded and then rushed after Melanie when she fled the room sobbing.

Adam pointed to Ted and me. "You needa go." He lowered his arm. "Done caused enough trouble." He turned and headed for the hallway.

"Do you think they'll be all right?" I asked Ted.

Susan had returned and had overheard my question. "I'll see to it that they are," she said. "I won't leave until Adam has passed out, and I'll call the cops if he gets violent."

"Thank you," Ted said. He looked at me. "We should go."

I nodded. "Susan, please, let us know if the Cantors need anything or if there's anything we can do."

On the drive to Captain Moe's, Ted was beating himself up over the incident at the Cantor home.

"If I hadn't said anything to Mary, Adam wouldn't have mouthed off and Melanie wouldn't have found out the truth about her grandfather's death," he said. "At least, she wouldn't have found out *that* way."

"Ted, you were only trying to offer assurances to Mary. It isn't your fault Adam is a drunken idiot." I paused. "He accused the police department of trying to frame him. Does that mean there's a pretty strong case against him?"

"You know I'm not at liberty to say," Ted said. "We're investigating all the possibilities."

"Off the record?"

He sighed. "Off the record, Adam has no solid alibi for the time of the murder. But I have a hard time believing he did it. I mean, I was there when he was told of his father's death. He looked genuinely shocked."

"So you don't feel Mary and Melanie are in any danger?" I asked.

"Sweetheart, they've been in danger for years. But at least now Adam knows he's being watched, and maybe that will temper his actions."

"Okay. Let's try to put the Cantors out of our

minds for a while and enjoy ourselves," I said, as Ted pulled into a parking space at Captain Moe's.

"I'm all for that." He shut off the engine and gave me a quick kiss before we got out of the car.

Captain Moe came to greet us as soon as we entered the diner. A bear of a man with a shock of white hair and a matching beard, he was as jovial as any Santa Claus ever depicted. He kissed my cheek and held out his hand to Ted. Ted had to let go of my hand to shake Captain Moe's.

"Oh, ho, ho!" Captain Moe laughed and winked at me. "I sense a change in the air." He put an arm around each of us and led us to a booth by a window. "Will the two of you be sharing a large plate of spaghetti like those Disney lovebirds?"

"We're not *Lady and the Tramp*!" I said in mock annoyance.

"No, my wee Tinkerbell, and I should be ashamed for likening you to a dog," Captain Moe said.

"We're more like *Beauty and the Beast*," Ted said.

Captain Moe put his fists on his hips. "You'd best not be calling my niece's godmother a beast, Detective Nash, or else I'll throw you out of my fine establishment!"

We all laughed, and then I asked Captain Moe how his niece, Riley, and her baby daughter, Laura, were doing.

"They're doing well. Riley is dreading her return

to work next week, but I don't know why—she's taking Laura right along with her. They've put a bassinette in the office."

"That's terrific," I said. "I'll have to drop in for a visit."

"Riley would like that," Captain Moe said. He turned to Ted. "Sad business about Chester Cantor."

A gaunt man of about fifty was walking past and stopped upon hearing Captain Moe's comment. "Chester Cantor? What happened to him?"

A flicker of irritation flashed across Captain Moe's broad face at the interruption before he turned and addressed the man. "Chester died yesterday, Ed."

"I'm real sorry to hear that." Ed wrinkled his brow. "I'd spoken with Chester not more than two weeks ago about helping him find some treasure he was looking for."

"What sort of treasure?" I asked.

Ed shrugged. "I dunno. Treasure he thought came from a ship called the *Delia* that sunk—oh, I reckon about two hundred years or more ago. He even showed me what he thought was a map pointing out where he believed the treasure was located."

"He had a map?" I asked.

Ed shook his head. "It wasn't a map in any real sense of the word. It looked like something somebody had embroidered."

"You mean, like a tapestry," I said.

"That's what he called it. It didn't look like any treasure map I'd ever seen." Ed shrugged as if he were an authority on treasure maps. "Poor old Chester. . . . He was desperate. And desperate people will do just about anything to get what they want." He clapped Captain Moe on the back. "See ya, Moe."

"Good-bye, Ed," Captain Moe said as Ed wandered off. He looked back at Ted and me. "Sorry for the intrusion."

"No problem," I said. "Do you think it's possible Chester Cantor's tapestry *was* a treasure map?"

"I imagine anything's possible, Tink," Captain Moe said. "But I think it's more likely that Chester was merely chasing rainbows like Ed said. Now, if he'd been looking for the lost Ramsey party gold, Sir Francis Drake's cache, or even the buried pirate treasure that was never fully recovered, then I might've taken this map talk more seriously. But I don't know of a single Oregonian—besides Chester—who ever thought there was any treasure to be found in the wreckage of the *Delia*."

"I really need to brush up on my Oregon history and find out more about all these treasures," I said with a grin.

After Captain Moe took our orders and went back to the counter, Ted arched his brow at me.

"What?" I asked.

He did a really lousy impression of my voice. " 'He had a *map*? Was it a *tapestry*?' "

"First of all, I sound nothing like that," I said. "And, two, we needed to find out more about what this Ed person knows about Chester and his map. I think he might be protesting a little too much about his belief that Chester's map was bogus. We should find out if he has an alibi for the time of Chester's murder."

He rolled his eyes. "Yes, Chief."

"Very funny."

"That's who you sounded like to me," Ted said, spreading his hands. "I think we'd better put this investigation on the back burner—the way *somebody* suggested—and enjoy our date."

Chapter Nine

Sunday was only a slightly overcast day, and since rain was forecast for the coming week, Ted and I took Angus to the beach. The two had already tired me out with their running, ball playing, and Frisbee tossing. I was stretched out on a lounge chair, watching them romp in the foamy waves, when my cell phone rang. I glanced at the screen and saw that it was Riley Kendall—Captain Moe's niece, new mom, and attorney extraordinaire.

I answered the call, "How does a busy woman like you find time to phone a lazy beach bum like me?"

"Au contraire, you've been pretty busy from what I hear."

I laughed. "Somebody's a tattletale."

"Uh-huh. Uncle Moe told me at church this morning that you and Ted are officially a couple," she said. "It's about time, is all I can say. You make a great team, and I believe you'll be happy together."

"Thank you," I said. "While I've got you on the phone, did you know Chester Cantor?"

"No, but Dad represented Adam on assault and destruction of personal property charges a few years back." Riley's dad, Norman Patrick, was formerly her law partner. He was currently serving time in a minimum-security prison for real estate fraud. "Adam got into a fight at the Brew Crew. He put one man in the hospital and totally trashed Todd's pub."

"I'd heard something about that," I said. "Sadie thinks Adam is meaner than a cobra with a toothache."

She chuckled. "I don't know that I'd go that far, but I do think Adam has an explosive temper."

"Would you imagine him being capable of murdering his father?" I asked.

"I'm not sure." She paused. "I don't think he'd do it on purpose—certainly not premeditated—but if he was angry enough, he might snap and not realize what he'd done until it was too late."

"That's why I'm so scared for his wife and daughter," I said.

Ted waved to me before Angus loped up to him and nearly knocked him down. I stifled a giggle and told Riley I'd stop by to see her and the baby sometime this week.

She warned me to be careful where Adam was

concerned. "You don't want that man's anger directed at you."

I promised to be extra cautious but stopped short of promising to stay out of Adam's business. If Mary or Melanie needed my help, I wouldn't hesitate to offer it. After ending the call, I dropped my phone into my beach tote and hurried to join Ted and Angus at the water's edge.

The weather was dreary, but my mood was sunny as I opened the door to the Seven-Year Stitch Monday morning. As I parked my dripping umbrella in the cast-iron stand and then hung my jacket in the office, Angus sniffed around until he'd found the Kodiak bear chew toy Vera had brought him a few weeks ago. He took the bear over to the window and began gnawing on its head.

"Jill, you're looking gorgeous as always," I said to the smiling mannequin. "I hope you had as good a weekend as Angus and I did."

I made sure all the bins and shelves were tidy and well stocked, and then I sank onto one of the red club chairs to work on Mom's Fabergé Easter egg. I hadn't stitched two full rows before she called me. Sometimes I believe that woman is psychic.

"Hey, Mom. I was just thinking about you."

"Were you? Or were you thinking of someone

more . . . I don't know . . . tall, dark, and handsome?" She spoke in a Mae West–inspired drawl that made me laugh.

"I really was thinking about you . . . and Easter."

"Maybe you and Ted could visit for Easter," she said. "Or maybe we could at least meet halfway or something. I miss you."

"I miss you too, Mom."

"All right, let's snap out of that before we get all sappy and maudlin. I called to see how your weekend went. Was it wonderful?"

"For the most part. Ted is dreamy. I'm so glad I decided to trust him with my heart. He even cooks!"

"Do tell."

I elaborated on the delicious meal he'd made us on Friday evening.

"You said your weekend was wonderful *for the most part*," she recalled, after saying that the dinner sounded scrumptious. "What wasn't so great about it?"

"Well, first, I ran into Todd at MacKenzies' Mochas after work Saturday," I said. "That was a little tough, but at least, I feel like we might be able to salvage our friendship."

"That's good. What about Sadie? Has she come around?" Mom asked.

"I haven't spoken with her since Friday."

"Do you think she's still upset? I mean, that's pretty extreme, don't you think?"

"It *is* extreme," I agreed. "I know she's close to Todd, but she and I have been best friends since college. And it's not like Ted is Adam Cantor." I told Mom about Adam throwing Ted and me out of his home Saturday night after we'd taken over the muffin basket and how—thanks to his angry outburst—Melanie found out her grandfather hadn't peacefully died in his sleep but had been murdered. "Plus, I spoke with Riley yesterday morning, and she's convinced Adam could've killed his father in a fit of rage."

"But that doesn't mean he did, love. Nor does it mean that he'll kill his wife and daughter."

"I get that, Mom. I do. But it still doesn't keep me from worrying about Mary and Melanie."

"What about the treasure map angle? Isn't there still the possibility that someone came into the home to steal the map and then killed Chester? Or has that been ruled out?"

"I don't think anything has been ruled out at this point," I said. "Plus, the deeper I dig on the subject of Oregon coast treasure, the more legends and speculations I turn up. So maybe that *is* what happened."

"What's your intuition telling you on this one?" she asked.

"I have no idea," I said. "I'm clueless."

"Oh, come on, now, my Nancy Drew. There are always clues. You'll find them."

"I hope so. Gotta run, Mom. A customer just came in. I'll talk with you again later."

"Be careful," she said. "I love you."

"Love you too."

When my customer took off her rain hat, I could see that she was Mary's friend Susan.

I smiled. "Good morning. Thanks for braving the weather to stop in. May I get you a cup of coffee?"

"No, thanks," she said, shrugging out of her slicker. "I can't stay too awfully long. I only wanted to give you an update on Mary and Melanie."

"Here. Let me take your jacket," I said.

She handed it to me, and I hung it on the rack in my office. "Are they doing all right?" I asked. "Are they still at home?"

"Yes, and yes." She sat on the sofa facing away from the window. "Adam seems to be treating them especially well right now."

"That's good."

"Yeah." She shrugged. "I don't expect it to last, but it's nice for the time being." She looked at the egg I was cross-stitching. There wasn't even enough of the pattern developed yet that anyone could tell what it was going to be, but she told me it was pretty.

"Thanks," I said with a smile. I showed her the pattern so she could get a better idea of what the finished product would look like.

"Ooh, that'll be beautiful," she said. "Did you ever see Chester's tapestry treasure map thing?"

I hesitated, struggling to come up with a suitable answer. I didn't want to tell Susan that for some inexplicable reason Chester had trusted me with his cherished tapestry. But I didn't want to appear to be hiding something either. "I understand he had a tapestry that he *believed* to be a treasure map. I'm just not sure that's what it was."

Susan's brows drew together sharply. "Why not? Why wouldn't it be a map? His mother told him it was."

"She might've only told her stubborn little boy what he needed to hear before agreeing to go to bed." I chuckled. "I'm not saying Chester's tapestry isn't a treasure map, but I'm skeptical about its veracity."

"So you don't think a ship called the *Delia* was wrecked off the coast of Tallulah Falls? Or you don't think the ship was carrying anything valuable?" she asked.

"I don't know about either of those things," I said, surprised at her adamant defense of Chester's map. "I only know that Chester Cantor was looking for a miracle."

"I agree," said Susan. "And I think he might've had a map to show him where he could find one."

"Then why hadn't he been looking for this treasure all his life?" I asked.

"I don't know. Maybe he had been. But there's a lot of treasure to be found here in Oregon—I know that. For instance, there's the treasure of Sir Frances Drake."

I recalled Captain Moe mentioning that, but I didn't comment on it to Susan.

"He buried five chests of gold," she continued. "Three were eventually found, but there are still two out there on the beach somewhere."

"It sounds like you're something of a treasure hunter yourself," I said.

"I sure would be if I knew where to look." She gazed at the far wall, making me feel as if she'd transported herself into an Indiana Jones or Lara Croft daydream. "I've heard the legends all my life . . . grew up reading the treasure hunters' books in the elementary school library . . . spent summers digging in the sand. . . ." She appeared to give herself a mental shake before rejoining the real world and giving me a sheepish smile. "Tell me, Marcy. What would you do if you stumbled upon a treasure?"

"I already have," I said, thinking of Ted. I suddenly remembered that Susan was in my Thursday evening class and that gushing over a boyfriend would be insensitive to a woman in a domestic abuse victims' support group. I nodded toward Angus. "Just look at him over there by the window. Isn't he adorable?"

"Oh, come on, I'm serious. What would you do with the money?"

"I'd pay off everything I owe, and then I'd hire someone to work here at the Seven-Year Stitch one day a week so I could take the day off and do whatever I wanted. What about you?" I asked.

"I'd start all over," Susan said. "I'd change my looks, buy a new wardrobe, and move to the other side of the country. Wouldn't that be fantastic?"

Once again, I hesitated to answer her. I knew what it was like to uproot oneself and make a fresh start in a new place. It was indeed liberating, but most of the problems you'd hoped to have left at your old place still accompanied you to the next. Then again, my problems probably hadn't been as huge as Susan's were. So I merely smiled and nodded.

Shortly thereafter, Susan bought a spool of wide red ribbon, said she'd see me in class on Thursday, and left—crouched over against the onslaught of rain.

As I continued working on Mom's egg, I debated the pros and cons of calling Sadie. While I had too much on my mind with the Cantors to dwell on Sadie's unreasonable anger or pouting or whatever she was feeling toward me, it was hard to put my best friend completely out of my mind when we'd last parted on such rocky ground. I mean, we'd been friends for years. Heck, I wouldn't have even opened my shop here in Tallulah Falls had it not been for Sadie. So, of course, the pro to calling her would be to smooth things over. And that would make the con the realization that I couldn't smooth things over if Sadie was still ticked off.

Fortunately, the debate was put on hold while I tended to a customer who was looking for a soft yarn that wouldn't pill when washed. I was ringing up the woman's purchase when Sadie walked in with a latte. She took a seat in the sit-and-stitch square, put the latte on the coffee table, and played ball with Angus until the customer and I had finished our transaction.

I was beginning to think maybe it wasn't Mom who was psychic. Maybe it was me.

I waved good-bye to the customer and then went to sit across from Sadie. "Hi," I said.

"Hi." She pushed the latte across the table toward me. "Low-fat vanilla with a hint of cinnamon."

"Thank you." I picked up the latte, opened it, and took a sip. It was nowhere near as hot as I'd expected it to be, and I wondered how long it had taken Sadie to fully make up her mind to come talk with me.

"Sorry about Friday," she said. "I was just disappointed about you and Todd. I thought you guys were a perfect fit." She tossed the tennis ball Angus had dropped at her feet, and he scampered after it. "You'd both been through so much heartache. I guess I thought you could heal each other's hurts."

I stayed silent and merely took another sip of the tepid latte. I didn't feel I had anything to add to what I'd already told Sadie on this touchy topic Friday.

"But I can see that Ted makes you happy," Sadie said. "And I'm glad."

I arched a brow and put the latte back on the coffee table. "Why do I get the feeling that Todd and Blake helped you arrive at that conclusion?"

"Because they did . . . Todd especially."

"He's a terrific guy," I said. "He's just not the right guy for me."

Sadie nodded. "I know." She stood. "Well, I'd better get back. Despite the rain—or maybe because of it—MacKenzies' Mochas is a madhouse today."

"I'm glad you took time to stop by," I said.

"Me too."

It wasn't a Laverne and Shirley or a Lucy and Ethel makeup scene, but it would do. Hopefully, we could double-date in the near future . . . and when Todd found a girl, even *triple* date. As I took the latte to reheat it in the microwave oven in my office, I decided I was getting way ahead of myself.

The bells over the shop door jingled, alerting me to the fact that someone had come in.

"Be right there!" I called.

"Take your time!"

I was a bit startled to have been answered by an unfamiliar male voice, so I stepped out of the office to investigate. It was Adam Cantor.

"Hi, Mr. Cantor," I said, hoping my voice didn't convey how ill at ease I was to find him standing in my store. "What can I do for you?"

"I'm here to apologize for my behavior Saturday evening," he said, absently patting Angus's head. He looked toward the sit-and-stitch square. "Do you have a second to talk?"

"Of course. Please, have a seat."

He strode to the farthest club chair and sat down, resting one ankle on the opposite knee.

Eager to keep some distance between us, I chose the other club chair.

"Mary, Melanie, and I appreciate the muffin basket you brought us," he told me. "That was very thoughtful."

"You're welcome," I said. "Blake from MacKenzies' Mochas said Melanie liked the chocolate, chocolate chip muffins, so he made sure to include several of those."

"Yeah, those are disappearing fast." Adam smiled. "Blake's a good guy. Again, I'm sorry I behaved so poorly Saturday evening. I'd been drinking a little . . . trying to drown my grief, I guess you could say, although it only made matters worse . . . and I lashed out at you and Detective Nash."

"The Tallulah Falls Police Department is doing its best to find out who murdered your father," I said.

"I know. But it won't bring him back, will it?" he asked. "Pop and I had lost the majority of my early years. I guess you could say we were trying to make up for lost time."

"I only met your father once, but during the brief time I spoke with him, he made it clear to me how much he loved his family."

"I didn't always treat him well," Adam said, softly, a slight catch in his voice.

Before I could stop myself, I said, "But you can make a concentrated effort to treat Mary and Melanie well."

His eyes narrowed. "What do you mean by that?"

You can get help to ensure you stop abusing your family is what I thought. My mind raced to come up with something more acceptable. To Adam, I said, "You just told me that you and your dad didn't make the most of your childhood. Your dad expressed regrets to me about that too." I lifted and dropped my shoulders—the ultimate gesture of casual offhandedness. "Being aware of those regrets can keep you from making the same mistakes your father made. It can encourage you to be the kind of dad and husband you wish he'd have been—and sooner in life rather than later. Right? Not that you aren't, I mean."

He still simply stared at me.

"After all," I continued, "didn't someone say, *A smart man learns from his own mistakes but a truly wise man learns from the mistakes of others*? I'm only saying that rather than grieve for the time you missed and the time you no longer have with your father, you can channel that energy into the time you have with your daughter and your wife so that you never have the regrets that plagued your dad."

"I see what you're saying," Adam said slowly. "Makes sense. Of course, I do want justice for my dad."

"Naturally. We all do."

"Why did he decide to confide in you when he hadn't even met you until you brought the books Friday morning?" he asked. "You hadn't met him before . . . had you?"

"Oh, no." I smiled. "I guess he was simply feeling chatty . . . and I just have one of those faces or something. People talk with me all the time."

"But why was he talking with you about me?"

"Um . . . I can't recall. We were just chatting in general when he said something about regretting not giving you the childhood you'd deserved." I shrugged. "I didn't pursue it."

He studied me for a moment as if trying to decide

whether or not I was telling the truth. "Do the police have any solid leads about who killed Pop?"

"I don't know," I said. "You should ask them."

"I have. They're being evasive."

Before he could elaborate, Reggie hurried into the shop. "Now, *this* is what I call a blustery day!" she said, smiling at Adam and me. "Hello, all. Marcy, I need three skeins each of white, silver, and blue perle floss, please."

"Excuse me," I said to Adam, as I got up and went over to Reggie. Angus was way ahead of me and was already sitting at her feet. "What shade of blue?" I asked.

"I'm not sure," Reggie said. "I'd better see what all you have."

"I should be going, but thank you again for your expression of sympathy, Marcy," Adam said, as he walked to the door.

"You're welcome," I said.

As soon as he left, Reggie confessed that she didn't really need any thread. "I was on my way to MacKenzies' Mochas when I noticed Adam in your shop and thought you might need my help. You don't think he caught wind of the escape plan, do you?"

"If so, he didn't let on," I said. "I think this was more of a fishing expedition."

Chapter Ten

Ted called before I left work that afternoon and said that Manu and Reggie had invited us for dinner. "Shall I accept?" he asked. "Or would you rather I politely decline?"

"No," I said. "I mean, please, accept. I think it'll be nice . . . unless you'd rather not go." I happened to think that Ted might not want to spend the evening with his boss.

"I'm fine with it. I just know Mondays and Fridays are your only free evenings during the week, and I thought you might have other plans."

"Nope. Just find out if they need us to bring anything," I said. "By the way, are you having a good day?"

"I am. Are you? When Reggie stopped in at the station earlier, she said Adam Cantor dropped in on you." Though he'd kept his tone light, there was an underlying hardness that told me he was concerned about the visit.

"He stopped in to apologize for his rude behavior Saturday evening . . . or, at least, that's what he said. I really think he was trying to find out what the police are doing with regard to Chester's murder."

"What did you tell him?" Ted asked.

"I told him I didn't know anything and that if he wanted information, he should ask the police," I said. "He told me you guys are being evasive. I guess that means that no one will come right out and tell him, *Congratulations! You're a suspect in your father's death!*"

"Well, we shouldn't have to beat him over the head with it," Ted said.

"You've never had any trouble convincing me I was a suspect."

"Is this where I say something horribly corny like *Yeah, but you're a thief—you stole my heart*?" he asked.

I laughed. "No. This is where you say *good-bye*, and I go home and get ready for our dinner date."

"Deal. Pick you up at six thirty?"

"Sounds great . . . but, please, leave the corn at home."

"I will," he promised.

Reggie had decorated the Singh home with the same eclectic blend of Indian and coastal decor with which she'd done her office at the library. And, once again, the effect was stunning. I had the feeling that if I—or almost anyone other than Reggie—had tried to pull off the look, it would've been a horrible failure.

The living room walls were painted a soft cream. The hardwood floor was covered with a large Indian rug that had shades of brown, blue, beige, and copper. A light blue sofa picked up the color from the rug, and two rattan rockers with matching ottomans had blue-and-copper-striped cushions. The end tables and the coffee table were glass-topped rattan. An elaborate painting hung on the wall directly across from the door. When I commented on it, Reggie told me it was the ceiling of the Taj Mahal.

"We bought it when we were there last," she said.

"Wow." I stepped over to take a closer look. "It's so intricate . . . and it's incredible how well it matches your living room."

"I know," Reggie said. "That's why I had to have it."

Manu took Ted's and my jackets and asked if we'd like drinks while we waited for dinner to finish cooking. I asked for water, and Ted said he didn't need anything.

We'd brought some white tulips as a hostess gift. Reggie went to put the flowers in a vase and said she'd bring the drinks back after she'd checked on dinner.

Manu invited us to sit down. He took one of the

rattan rockers, and we sat on the sofa. Like their decor, he and his wife had very different styles that
meshed delightfully. While Reggie preferred traditional Indian dress, like the black and gold tunic she
wore this evening, Manu chose a more American
style. Like Ted and me, he wore jeans. But where the
two of us were wearing lightweight sweaters, Manu
wore a blue plaid flannel shirt. He had a fondness
for flannel shirts. Reggie teasingly referred to them
as his lumberjack duds.

"Reggie told Ted and me that Adam Cantor came
to your shop today," Manu said. "He didn't threaten
you in any way, did he?"

"No," I said. "He was actually pretty nice. Of
course, as I told Reggie, I think he was hoping I
could tell him something about his father's murder
investigation, but he hit a brick wall there."

Manu nodded. "That's what Reggie said. She was
so afraid he'd found out that the bookmobile wasn't
the real reason you'd paid a visit to his house."

Reggie returned with a tray of drinks—white
wine for her and Manu, and water for Ted and me.
"In case you change your mind," she told Ted. "And
if either of you decides you'd like a glass of wine,
please, let me know."

"I'll wait and have mine with dinner," I said. "But
thank you."

"I heard Adam Cantor's name," she said to Manu,

as she placed the tray on the coffee table and handed him his drink. She took her own glass and sat on the other rattan rocker.

"I was telling Marcy you were afraid Adam had discovered that you, Reggie, and Audrey had been hoping to talk Chester into leaving rather than bringing books to a shut-in," Manu said.

"Well, Chester did check out a couple of books. . . ." She trailed off and looked at me. "But that doesn't change the fact that Adam was duped . . . and that he was duped in order for us to get in there and talk his family into leaving him. Still, if anyone should bear the brunt of his anger over that, it should be me. I'm sorry I dragged you and Audrey into this, Marcy."

"If I'm not mistaken, going to the Cantor house in the bookmobile was my idea," I said.

"And I've never known Marcy to have to be *dragged* into anything that was none of her business," Ted teased.

I playfully elbowed him in the side.

"That's true," Reggie said.

"Hey! What is this?" I asked. "Gang up on Marcy night?"

"You didn't let me finish," Reggie said, with a laugh. "It is true, but I knew your heart would go out to the women in that group." She turned serious again. "I shouldn't have taken you to the Cantors' house. Mary could've brought the tapestry to you, had she wanted you to assess its worth for Chester."

"She could have, but I really enjoyed meeting him," I said.

Sensing the downward turn of my mood, Ted asked, "So, how did the women in the group take to embroidery?"

"I think most of them are enjoying the class," I said. "In fact, one of them—Mary's friend Susan—stopped by the Seven-Year Stitch for the second time today."

"Susan Willoughby?" Reggie asked. She sipped her wine. "She's an odd one."

"I suppose her last name is Willoughby," I answered. "I thought I was doing well to remember her first name since there are so many women in the group. She *is* the only Susan in the class, isn't she?"

Reggie nodded. "Medium height, sandy blond hair, brown eyes?"

"That's the one," I said. "Why did you say she's an odd one?"

"She seems to be more of an observer than a participant," Reggie said. "They all are at first, but eventually most of the women begin to trust one another, commiserate, and open up about their experiences. Not Susan."

"Wait." Manu held out his hand. "Susan Willoughby is in the domestic abuse victims' support group?"

When Reggie confirmed that she was, Manu asked why.

As Reggie shrugged, I looked from her to Manu to Ted.

"I thought the group was comprised of women from the safe house and those living in at-risk situations," I said. "Not that I mind having her in the class or anything, but why would Susan be in the group if she wasn't a victim of domestic abuse?"

"Maybe she comes to lend her support to Mary," Ted said.

"Or it could be that she *is* a survivor and feels she can help others get through it," Reggie said. "She certainly hasn't put herself in that role yet, though."

Manu shook his head. "I know Jared Willoughby. No way is he a wife beater."

"You can't know that for sure," Reggie said. "Some people are adept at hiding their true selves from the public."

"Not Jared," said Manu. "He's a stand-up guy."

"I'm not saying he isn't." Reggie took another sip of her wine. "I'm only pointing out that you never truly know someone until you're living with them."

"And maybe not then," I said lightly. "Anyone remember the story "Button, Button" by Richard

Matheson? It's the one where the couple was to receive fifty thousand dollars if they pressed a button. The catch was that someone the button-presser did not know would die."

"I remember," said Ted. "The wife pressed the button, and her husband died in an accident. He had a twenty-five-thousand-dollar life insurance policy. . . ."

"*With a double indemnity clause*," we finished in unison, laughing. The insurance company had paid the wife fifty thousand dollars because it paid double the amount of the policy if the death was accidental.

"But you said the person who died would be someone they didn't know," Reggie said.

"The catch was that the wife only *thought* she knew her husband," I said.

"That's a scary thought," she said.

"Don't worry," Manu said. "You know me better than I know myself."

When Ted and I got back to my house, I made us a pot of decaf while Ted let Angus in and fed him treats.

"Dinner was fun," I said, as I took two mugs out of the cabinet and placed them on the counter.

"Yes, it was." Ted came up behind me, slid his

arms around my waist, and kissed my neck. "The meal wasn't what I expected, though."

"It wasn't?" I giggled. "It was almost *exactly* what I expected. I mean, I didn't know what foods Reggie would serve, but I knew she'd have a mix of Indian and American dishes."

Reggie had treated us to oven-baked barbecue chicken with vegetable curry, rolls, and a yummy pudding called *kheer*.

"I guess we could call Reggie's cooking style American-Indian cuisine, but then that would mean something else entirely," he murmured against the back of my neck. "Wouldn't it?"

"Mmm-hmm." I closed my eyes and sank back against him.

"I feel your resistance to my charms beginning to weaken," he said, turning me to face him.

"Silly man." I wrapped my arms around him. "I never had any resistance to your charms."

He lowered his lips to mine, and we were enjoying a deliciously hot kiss until Angus wedged himself between us.

"Dude, gimme a break," Ted said to Angus. "You get to be with her all day."

"True, but he doesn't get to be with *you*." I poured our coffee, and we took it into the living room.

Angus happily padded after us. When we slipped

off our shoes and snuggled up on the sofa, the dog was content to lie nearby and chew on a toy.

Curled against Ted with my head resting on his chest, I felt happier than I could remember feeling in years. I told him so.

He kissed me lightly. "Me, too, sweetheart. In fact, I think the only other thing I need right now is to find Chester Cantor's murderer and get him off the street so I won't have to worry about Adam harassing you."

"Adam Cantor doesn't scare me," I lied. "I've got my own personal bodyguard twenty-four-seven, remember?"

We both looked over at Angus, and he wagged his tail in acknowledgment before resuming the all-important business of toy chewing.

"You've seen Chester's tapestry treasure map," I said. "Which do you think it is—a tapestry or a treasure map?"

He shrugged and nestled me closer. "I think it's a tapestry designed to look like a treasure map." He ran his finger along my collarbone. "What do you think?"

"I have no idea, but I know that a lot of people around Tallulah Falls have a burning desire to find treasure."

"It's like our answer to the lottery. Everybody

wants to win big." He kissed the trail his fingertip had forged along my collarbone. "Now, burning desire . . . that's a feeling I'm familiar with."

"Come on," I said. "Be serious for just a second."

"I *am* serious." He lifted his head. "Okay—one second . . . not a minute more. I say anything's possible."

"Really? You think the tapestry could actually lead to the discovery of the wreckage of the *Delia*?"

"Why not? Like I said, anything's possible," he said. "Now, time's up and your so-called bodyguard is snoring. Come here."

Since I was about to lose my train of thought in a pair of the bluest eyes I'd ever seen anyway, I put aside the plan that was forming somewhere in the recesses of my mind. And then I kissed Ted and showed him that he wasn't the only one who knew a thing or two about burning desire.

Chapter Eleven

The next morning, I looked at the photos I'd taken of Chester's tapestry and had uploaded from my phone to my computer. I printed them out, pieced them together, and pinned them to the bulletin board in my office so I could look at the tapestry as a whole. To be on the safe side, I got a piece of green felt from the storage room to tack over the photos in case anyone happened to walk in. It would be just my luck for someone to see the board and deduce that I'd killed Chester Cantor to get at his treasure.

I stood back and surveyed the photos. Was it possible that this lovely old piece of embroidery held the key to finding a sunken treasure? There were longitude and latitude indicators . . . an X where the *Delia* had apparently sunk . . . towns—including Tallulah Falls—along the shoreline. . . .

I was so caught up in my reverie that when Angus suddenly began barking, I gasped and nearly jumped a foot off the ground. I threw the felt over the bulletin board and then hurried to see what all the commotion was about.

It was a bird. That's it . . . just a tiny sparrow that was pecking on the window. Angus was dying to play with it. He was in front of the window with his head down at bird level and his wagging tail up in the air while he barked a blue streak.

When I could no longer take Angus's and the bird's shenanigans—in particular, Angus's loud barks and playful rumbles—I went to the counter and retrieved his leash and the cardboard clock with the plastic hands that told the world that I was out but that I would be back at the indicated time. I placed the hands five minutes in the future, placed the clock on the door, snapped the leash to Angus's collar, and we went for a quick jaunt down the street. As we walked, the scheme that had started forming in my brain last night fully awoke and began turning into a full-fledged plan.

When Angus and I got back to the Seven-Year Stitch, I waited on a customer who was making a needlepoint rug and needed strong yarn and tapestry needles. And *then* I called the treasure hunter, Jack Powell. He answered on the first ring. I introduced myself and then got right down to business.

"Jack, do you honestly believe Chester Cantor's map could lead us to the *Delia*?"

"I thought I made that clear to you the other day," he told me. "There's a better-than-passing average that the map could've led us to the wreckage, but with no map and no money, it doesn't do us any good to dwell on it."

"What if I said I might be able to get my hands on the map *and* the money?" I asked. "Would you be interested in spearheading the hunt?"

For a moment, he didn't answer. Then he asked in almost a whisper, "Are you serious?"

"I am. I can't promise anything yet," I said. "But if I'm able to get the funding, would you head up the search team?"

"You bet I would," he said. "But wait. What's in it for you?"

"Chester's share—I want it to go to his family."

"If there's anything to divvy up, I'll be glad to pass along a share to the Cantors," Jack said. "How sure are you that you can make this happen?" There was a note of excitement creeping into his voice.

"On a scale of one to ten, I'd say, four point seven five," I answered. I realized those weren't great odds, but I didn't want to get his hopes up too high in case my plan failed. "Let me make some calls, and I'll get back in touch with you as soon as I have something more concrete."

Since reality television had become such a major part of almost every network, I thought the hunt for the *Delia*'s treasure might be of interest to someone. Even if no treasure was found, a documentary film crew might finance the search and would pay the Cantors for their role in the film—the story behind Chester's tapestry, the use of the tapestry/map to try to locate the treasure. . . . Even Chester's assertion that his ancestors were the Ramsays of Oregon treasure lore could provide interesting fodder for viewers. It might not be the windfall Chester had hoped for, but at least it would be something . . . maybe enough to put in a trust for Melanie's college education.

The rain from yesterday had abated to a light mist today, and a lot more customers were out and about. That was wonderful for business, but it was terrible for sneaking off to my office to make phone calls. After speaking with Jack Powell, it was over an hour before I was able to get a few minutes to call Mary Cantor.

Unlike Jack, Mary did not answer on the first ring. In fact, I was afraid I was going to have to give up when at last she answered.

"Mary, hi. It's Marcy Singer. Can you talk?"

"Yes, Marcy. Adam is out at the moment. If my tone changes, you'll know he's come in and that I have to go," Mary said.

"Of course. I . . . I don't mean to be insensitive here, but Chester indicated that you and Adam have . . . had . . . money issues?" This call went better in my head before I'd actually dialed the number.

"I don't see that our financial situation is any of your business." Mary's voice was cool.

"It isn't in the least," I agreed. "It's just that I've been studying photographs I took of the tapestry, and there's a slight possibility that it really could be a treasure map. Certainly, the tapestry is old."

"Marcy, I don't really think this is the proper time to get everybody's hopes up for something that will never be. Do you?"

"No." I forged ahead. "But it could be the perfect time to get out from under your financial burden. You know how reality shows are all the rage? Well, what if we could get a producer interested in finding the treasure of the *Delia*?"

Mary sighed. "You said there was a *slight* possibility that the tapestry is a treasure map. If that isn't the case, then what?"

"Then the production company might still be interested in making a documentary or a reality show about searching for the treasure," I said. "Wouldn't it at least be worth a shot?"

"I don't know. What are the odds that anyone would listen to this idea for a show?" she asked.

"Oh, trust me. I believe I can get the right people

to listen. And if I can, would you be interested in talking with them?"

"Sure." Her voice changed, indicating Adam had returned. "Adam and I do so appreciate your concern. Thank you for calling."

After getting Mary's green light, I called Mom. "Mom, I need a favor."

"Marcella, what's wrong?"

"Nothing," I said quickly. "Remember that treasure map tapestry I told you about?"

"The one that possibly got Chester Cantor killed? Yes, I remember your mentioning that," Mom said. "I'm sitting. Should I lie down?"

"If you think it would help," I said. "I'm calling to ask if you know a documentary filmmaker who might be willing to finance the treasure hunt?"

"Ah, that wasn't as bad as I thought it would be," she said, relief evident in her voice. "I'm not sure what I imagined you might be doing with regard to this treasure that may or may not be at the bottom of the ocean, but you're actually making a reasonable request."

"I doubt everyone around here will share your opinion, but we'll see."

"I'm drawing a blank on filmmakers, darling, but there's a new network called Explore Nation that's launching next year," Mom said. "Your proposal should be perfect for them."

"Do you have an in?"

"As a matter of fact, I do have an in—a rather powerful in. He's a major investor in the network. Let me give him a call and see what he thinks."

"Thanks, Mom. You rock!"

"I do, don't I?" She chuckled. "I'll keep you posted."

After talking with Mom, I'd wanted to call Ted and tell him my plan. But, as had been par for the course today, a steady stream of customers and phone calls had made it impossible to do so. That's why I was especially delighted to see him strolling in with lunch at a little past noon. He sat on the sofa while I checked out a customer who was buying knitting needles in a variety of sizes but no yarn, an oddity I might've commented on, had I been less busy. And then I waited on a customer who was buying a beaded embroidery kit for his wife.

As the last customer was heading out the door, I sprinted over to Ted and threw my arms around his neck. "I'm so glad to see you! I've been wanting to talk with you all morning."

"Ditto. Has the Stitch been a madhouse all day?"

"It has been," I said.

He nodded toward the bag. "I brought subs and chips. I'll mind the store while you go eat. You need a break."

I gave him a quick kiss. "Thanks for the offer, but I want to eat with you. My customers can spare me for twenty minutes." I put the clock on the door, and then Ted, Angus, and I went into the office.

"I brought tuna salad for you, turkey for me, and roast beef for Angus," Ted said.

"You brought Angus his own sub?" I asked. "How sweet."

"Those compelling eyes kill me. And I'm pretty hungry, so I figured if I had to share anyway, I might as well get him his own."

I laughed and hoped my compelling eyes would work on him as well when I confessed what I hoped to accomplish with regard to the search for the treasure of the *Delia*.

Ted stopped right in the middle of taking our food from the bag. "What?" he asked.

"What do you mean *what*?"

"You know exactly what I mean. What have you done?"

"You didn't make head detective just because of your good looks, did you?" I smiled.

Ted did not smile. He looked apprehensive.

"Hear me out," I continued.

He groaned and slapped a hand to his forehead.

"Please," I said.

"Okay." He lowered his hand, but he still looked like he dreaded what was coming.

"It's not that bad. Seriously," I said. "It's just that I got to thinking that Chester's tapestry might be worth something—a lot even—whether it's a map leading to the discovery of a sunken treasure or not."

"You mean the tapestry itself . . . because it's an antique?" Ted asked. He looked relieved.

"Not exactly."

Ted's look of relief disappeared.

"I mean, I did look into that," I said. "But it isn't worth as much as you might think. Anyway, you know how hot reality shows are, right?"

He nodded and started unwrapping his sandwich. Angus licked his lips and inched closer.

I explained about the television network set to launch next year and how Mom said she'd ask one of the network executives about doing a documentary on the search for the treasure. "Even if it's a bust like that time Geraldo Rivera opened Al Capone's vault, it could still make for some interesting television. Don't you think?"

Ted's eyes widened. "You're having your mom pitch the treasure hunt to a TV network?"

I nodded. "And Jack Powell has agreed to head up the expedition. So, provided the network goes for it, and they need a treasure hunter, we're good to go."

His jaw dropped. "Are you serious?"

"Yeah! Isn't it great? I figure this plan—if the network goes for it—will accomplish two things. First,

it will bring in some money for Chester's family . . .
maybe not as much as he'd hoped, but some. And, if
the tapestry was the reason Chester was killed, this
will draw out the murderer."

"And you think that's a good thing?"

"Of course," I said. "Don't you?" I unwrapped
my sub and took a bite. "Mmm . . . this is terrific.
Thank you."

"You're welcome." He shook his head. "What
does any of this have to do with Geraldo Rivera and
Al Capone's vault?"

"Nothing really. I only brought up that show to
illustrate that people will tune in to something even
if it turns out to be a disappointment." I grabbed two
sodas from the mini-fridge and placed them on the
desk. "See, back in 1986, Geraldo Rivera opened Al
Capone's secret vault beneath the Lexington Hotel
in Chicago. Rivera was so certain there was going to
be some super-creepy stuff in there that he even had
a medical examiner on hand in case there were human remains. Turned out, the vault's contents were
far less exciting than anticipated."

"What was in there?" Ted asked.

"Trash, mostly."

He laughed. "And you know all this because . . . ?"

"Because it's legendary in the movie and TV business," I said. "And even though the program itself
was an epic failure, it proved that people will tune in

to shows like that . . . out of curiosity if nothing else. Look at some of the garbage that passes for TV shows these days. Don't you think a documented hunt for sunken treasure would be more entertaining than some of those?"

"I do." He tore a hunk off the roast beef sub and handed it to Angus. "I just don't know how you're going to pull this off."

"Well, I might not. I mean, if the network isn't interested, then I guess that's that." I shrugged. "But if they are interested, then I'll talk with Mary again—and include Adam this time—and—"

"*We'll* talk with Mary and Adam," he interrupted. "I don't want you talking to that man without me. I don't believe he killed Chester, but I don't doubt that he's dangerous."

"Okay." I sipped my soda. "This could turn out to be a good thing. Wait and see."

Ted merely grinned tightly before taking a bite out of his sub. He didn't seem to have much confidence in my plan, but I really thought it could work.

At around three o'clock that afternoon, I got a call from "John Trammel, but everybody calls me J.T."

That was the extent of his introduction so I said, "Hi, J.T. What can I do for you?"

"Well, it appears your mother put a bug in my

boss's ear, and now he's all fired up about us going on a treasure hunt."

"You're with Explore Nation," I said excitedly. "So we're really doing it?"

He chuckled—a rich, robust laugh that, along with his Texas twang, made me think J. T. Trammel was a hearty man.

"I don't know how much literal involvement you'll have," he said. "But I'll be down your way first thing tomorrow morning to get all the particulars from you and to, hopefully, start the ball rolling if this proves to be a project we're interested in pursuing further."

"That's great," I said. "Just tell me when and where you'd like to meet and what you'd like for me to bring to the meeting."

"Ed—my boss—said Bev told him that you have some sort of shop there in Tallulah Falls," J.T. said.

"I do. It's an embroidery specialty shop called the Seven-Year Stitch."

"All right. What do you say we meet there at nine? I'll bring my assistant, Stacey, to mind the store while we chat."

"Nine it is," I said. "And I don't think the assistant will be necessary. The shop doesn't open until ten, so we'll have an hour undisturbed."

"I'll bring her anyway. We might run long."

"Anything else?" I asked.

"Your mom told Ed you have photos of the map. Is that right?"

"Yes. As a matter of fact, I have them pinned to the bulletin board in my office."

"Good," he said. "Also, dig up as much information on the ship and the shipwreck that you can for me."

"I'll do that."

"Nice talking with you, Marcy. I'm looking forward to our face-to-face in the morning."

"So am I."

As soon as I hung up, I called Mom. "You work fast," I told her.

"It's easy when you know what strings to pull. Fill me in."

I explained about the call from J. T. Trammel. "He's not wasting any time, Mom. He's meeting with me tomorrow morning at nine."

"That's terrific," she said. "I hope this works out for you."

"I hope it works out for the Cantors . . . in more ways than one. More than anything, I believe Chester wanted his son to stop mistreating his family." I sighed. "I wish I had the courage to tell that to Adam Cantor."

I heard Mom's sharp intake of breath. "Tread cautiously there, darling. Men like Adam Cantor don't like to be told they're *wrong*. And they detest the very hint of being accused of wrong*doing*."

"Don't worry," I said. "I'm not about to do anything that stupid. He'd just deny it anyway. But maybe somehow all this will make him take a long, hard look at his life."

Chapter Twelve

After work, I closed up the shop and left the cardboard clock on the door assuring my students I'd be back for class at six o'clock. I took Angus home and had just fed him when Ted arrived.

"Hi," I said, giving Ted a kiss and a hug. "Come on into the kitchen."

"I thought I'd drop in on my way home from work and see if you'd heard anything from the network people," he said.

"As a matter of fact, I did." I told him about my call from J. T. Trammel. "We're meeting at nine at the shop tomorrow morning." I opened the refrigerator door. "Would you like a soda?"

"Please."

I handed Ted a regular soda and took a diet soda for myself. "Mr. Trammel wants me to dig up everything I can find on the *Delia*," I said, uncapping my bottle and sitting down at the kitchen table.

Ted pulled out the chair across from me and sat down. "Since you have class tonight, I can go ahead and start your research, if you'd like for me to."

"I'd love that," I said. "I already have a lot of stuff about the *Delia* that I gathered while I was checking into the possible legitimacy of Chester's tapestry. It's mainly Web links and notes. The information is on a travel drive I take back and forth between my office at work and the one here."

Angus scratched at the door, and I got up and let him out into the fenced backyard. While I was up, I got the travel drive from my purse and handed it to Ted.

"Would you like for me to work here?" he asked. "That way, we can compile our notes for Mr. Trammel when you get home."

"That would be fantastic, and I know Angus will love the company. I'll bring home Chinese food." I had another thought. "Would you like to join me at the meeting with Trammel?"

He grinned. "I thought you'd never ask."

"I started to call Mary to see if she'd like to come, but I felt I should get Trammel's thoughts on the project first," I said. "He might look at it and decide not to do it. I wouldn't want to get Mary's hopes up just to have to watch them crash."

*   *   *

I got back to the Seven-Year Stitch at about twenty minutes before six. I unlocked the door, put the cardboard clock by the cash register, and began gathering the materials students would need for their first introductory candlewick embroidery class. I had an index card with some fun facts about candlewick embroidery, or "candlewicking"—such as, how the technique got its name (from the fact that the Colonial women who developed it used the same thread for the embroidery projects as they used to make wicks for their candles). I also had handouts for the students giving them step-by-step instructions on making a Colonial knot. While I'd be helping them there in class, they might need a refresher when they got home. And once they mastered the Colonial knot, they were pretty much home free in candlewick embroidery.

I went into the office to brew a pot of decaffeinated coffee and to make sure the mini-fridge was amply stocked with bottled water. As I got the coffee under way and was opening the cabinet to get a bag of hard candy, I heard the bells over the shop door ring.

I stepped out of the office with the bag of candy and was surprised to see Mary Cantor and Susan Willoughby standing near the counter. They hadn't signed up for this class, and at first, I thought they'd confused this class with their group class.

"Hi, guys," I said, carrying the bag of hard candy over to the round bowl in the center of the coffee table. I filled the dish with candy.

"Are we too early?" Mary asked.

"Not if you're here for beginning candlewick embroidery," I said lightly. "But if you're here for our other class—the cross-stitch and needlepoint class—you're two days early and in the wrong place."

"Oh, we know," Mary said. "We wanted to talk with you . . . and since you were so nice to come by with the muffin basket and all, Adam gave me permission to take your class." She looked behind her as if he might suddenly burst through the door. "He doesn't know about the other class, of course."

Of course, he didn't. And how *sweet* of him to give her permission to take this class.

"I realize we didn't register for the class ahead of time," Susan said. "If that's a problem—"

"Not at all," I interrupted. "The more, the merrier, right?" I smiled. "Please, excuse me and make yourselves comfortable while I put this candy bag back in the office. Would you guys care for some decaf coffee or a bottle of cold water?"

Susan said water would be nice, and Mary followed me into the office.

"Um . . . if you have a second, could I talk with

you after class?" she asked. "I know the other people will be coming soon. . . ."

As if on cue, the bells were set to jangling.

"Sure," I said.

She thanked me and started to leave the office when she noticed the bulletin board. Fortunately, the green felt was in place and completely covered the photos of Chester's tapestry.

"What's that?" Mary asked.

"It's a bulletin board," I said, keeping my voice as casual as I could.

"Why is it covered up like that?"

"Sometimes when I'm working on something . . . you know, like a surprise . . . I'll cover up my notes or sketches or whatever in case someone should come by . . . and spoil the surprise," I said.

It sounded lame even to me, even though it *was* a valid concept. I should've said something less vague . . . something to the effect that I was working on a special gift for someone and was afraid she might come in and see my preliminary work. That was much closer to the truth, after all, but I was afraid that if I'd said that, Mary would ask more questions. As it was, I didn't have time to explain to her—nor did I want to risk Susan overhearing—that the felt hid photos of Mary's late father-in-law's tapestry and that they were going to be evaluated by a production crew tomorrow morning. I was still afraid that Mr. Trammel might decide the *Delia* wasn't worth his time after all and nix the project before it had even begun.

Gee, I wished I'd put more thought into this plan while it was in its infancy. I'm not certain I'd have done anything differently. I only wish I'd have given it a little more thought prior to rushing into a meeting with a producer.

"Is anything wrong?" Mary asked.

It was a reasonable question. I was standing there with a dazed expression on my face and a bag of hard candy clutched in both hands. I probably looked a little deranged.

I shook myself out of it and smiled. "I'm fine." I put the candy into the cabinet and got two bottles of water out of the fridge—one for Susan and the other for me. I asked Mary again if she'd care for anything, but she said no.

We went out into the shop to see who else had arrived.

Vera was there. She was always game for trying something new. Reggie was there too. Like Vera, Reggie enjoys new ventures. But since Reggie is skilled in the art of *chikankari*, an Indian form of white-on-white embroidery, I wondered if she hadn't signed up for this class as either a thank-you for my doing the domestic abuse victims' group class or to make sure

Adam Cantor didn't come in during the session to do me bodily harm.

Once everyone who'd signed up for the class arrived, I gave an introductory speech on candlewick embroidery. I explained to the class that although more modern candlewick pieces often incorporated colored threads, we would be sticking with the traditional white-on-white motif for our class. I also passed around the Colonial knot instruction guide and the patterns we'd be using. Then I had everyone introduce herself to the class.

Besides Mary, Susan, Vera, and Reggie, there were Martha, a ski instructor; Belinda, a retired teacher; Amy, a court reporter who'd learned about the Seven-Year Stitch from Riley Kendall—I made a mental note to thank Riley; and Ellen, a full-time caregiver to her aging mother. Ellen's children had signed her up for this class as a way of getting her to do something for herself, and they'd agreed to take turns sitting with their grandmother so Ellen could enjoy her leisure time.

We were all telling Ellen what a sweet gift her children had given her and how glad we were that she was with us when Sadie hurried in.

"Hi," she said breathlessly. "Am I too late to join the class?"

Sadie was not a stitcher. A few weeks ago, she'd

signed up for beginning needlepoint and gotten frustrated halfway through the class, and I'd had to complete her project for her. I knew that her joining this class was a way of reaching out to me and letting me know we were okay.

"You're right on time," I said, giving her the handouts and a hug.

The class went well. Everyone seemed to enjoy it, and it appeared they'd all got the hang of the Colonial knot by the end of the session. Before I knew it, our class time was up. Once again, I found myself alone with Mary and Susan. I'd started cleaning up as the students began to leave, but after everyone else had left, I sat on the sofa across from Mary and Susan and asked what they wanted to talk with me about.

Mary's eyes darted toward the door before she answered. "It's about Adam."

Her voice was barely above a whisper, and I had to lean forward and fully concentrate on hearing her. "What about him?" I asked, not sure I wanted to know the answer to that question.

"Do the police think he killed Chester?" Her eyes glistened with fear and unshed tears.

"I don't know," I said. "I don't think they can clear anyone as a suspect at this point, but I believe Adam is genuinely grieving the loss of his father. That doesn't sound much like a murderer to me."

"I hope you're right," Mary said.

"Still, I heard his alibi didn't hold up," Susan said.

I started to ask Susan where she'd gotten her information, but I didn't. Instead, I said, "I'm positive the police are following every lead." I wondered if Susan was convinced that Adam had indeed killed Chester or if she merely wanted Mary to be cautious of him. I didn't think Mary needed anyone to make her wary of Adam. I could tell she was terrified of the man.

I wanted to be reassuring, but I couldn't be certain Adam was *not* the murderer. And if I were Mary and had any inkling that the man I was living with could kill someone—especially his own father—I wouldn't want to stay with him, and I certainly wouldn't want my daughter living under the same roof with him. But I didn't want to sway Mary into leaving her husband either. There could still be a chance for the Cantors to mend their family. I wanted to help foster that chance if I could, not take it away.

My mind was so muddled I barely remembered to stop and get the Chinese food on the way home. I was more than ready to simply fall into Ted's arms and hide when I got there.

He took the take-out boxes from me, put them on the table, and held me tight.

"Don't let go," I whispered. "Not yet."

"I won't. Is anything wrong? Did something happen?"

I buried my face in his chest. "Give me a second. We'll talk while we eat, but for the moment, I only want to escape here in your arms. You make me feel safe."

"You are safe, sweetheart." He rested his cheek against the top of my head. "I promise."

"You're probably starving," I said.

"Dinner can wait."

I smiled up at him. "You're wonderful. Thank you for being here."

He kissed me tenderly. "That must've been some rough class."

I laughed softly. "It's not *that* particular class I'm concerned about." I reluctantly stepped out of the warmth of his arms and got us some plates.

While we ate and fed bites of the sweet and sour pork to Angus, I told Ted about Mary and Susan coming to the class and staying to talk with me afterward.

"Everyone seems to think I know exactly what's going on with the investigation," I said. "And, in fact, I'm as clueless as they are . . . if not more so."

"That's a side effect of being involved with me," Ted said. "Sorry about that."

"I'm not sorry about that in the least." I took his hand. "I was so torn, Ted. I didn't know what to say. She was essentially asking me if I thought she and her daughter were living with a murderer . . . if I believe their lives are in danger. And I had no idea what to say to her. What do you tell people when they ask you those kinds of questions?"

"I think you handled the situation the only way you could," he said. "Like you, I see both sides of the coin. I want to protect Mary and Melanie, but I don't want to condemn Adam if he's innocent. Besides, domestic abuse statistics show that women who leave their abusive spouses are at a greater risk of severe injury or death than those who stay."

I groaned. "I want a rewind button. I want to go back to when I agreed to do the class and tell Reggie I'm too busy. I want to have never gotten involved with any of this." I pressed my lips together tightly, hoping that might somehow keep me from crying. It didn't work. "If I'd stayed out of it . . . hadn't gone meddling in the Cantors' business . . . Chester might still be alive. . . . He might be fine right now . . . searching for his treasure."

"Shh . . . come on, now." Ted stood and gently led me into the living room, where he sat on the sofa and cradled me on his lap.

"Do you think there's any hope for them?" I asked. "Is it possible Adam will stop being abusive to Mary and Melanie and be a good husband and father like Chester had hoped?"

"Probably not without help," he said. "He has to admit he needs help and then get it before any true change can occur."

"And that isn't likely, is it?" I asked glumly.

"Anything is possible. I do believe Chester had the right idea—get the family out and then offer Adam a way to receive help so the family can heal and come back together." He shrugged. "Maybe your getting Explore Nation involved will give Chester's dream a shot."

"That's what I'd hoped to do. But now I'm even second-guessing that." I told Ted about my worry that after talking with Mary about it and getting her to thinking the production could solve their money problems, Explore Nation would bail.

"So let's put together a compelling proposal for Mr. Trammel and see what happens," Ted said. "Then we'll take it from there."

"You're so good for me," I said.

He grinned and shook his head. "*You're* good for *me*." He jerked his head toward the stairs and my home office. "Let's get to work on that proposal."

Chapter Thirteen

I pulled into my usual spot near the Seven-Year Stitch, and Ted parked behind me. I'd left Angus at home this morning, hoping I'd have time to go back and get him after the meeting with Trammel. I hopped out of the Jeep and locked the doors using my key fob. I anxiously waited for Ted to get out of his car and join me on the sidewalk. Thankfully, it was overcast but not raining . . . at least, not yet.

"Do I look all right?" I asked. I'd worn a peacock blue, long-sleeved wrap dress and taupe pumps. Now I was worried that I was too casual . . . or maybe not casual enough. Should I have worn a suit? Or jeans, boots, a turtleneck, and a blazer?

"You look beautiful," Ted said.

His voice barely penetrated the frenzied thoughts zipping through my mind. Naturally, he looked super. He was wearing what he'd wear to work anyway—a navy suit, white shirt, and blue-and-gray-striped tie. He reminded me of that gorgeous guy from the show *White Collar*.

"And what about coffee?" I asked, as I unlocked the door. "Should I wait until they get here and then order from MacKenzies' Mochas? Or should I put a pot on to brew so that waiting for coffee won't hold up our meeting?"

"Put on a pot to brew. The aroma will be welcoming."

"Brilliant." I gave him a quick squeeze. "What else?"

Ted glanced at his watch. "Let's get our presentation set up. They might be early."

He was absolutely right. We'd arrived twenty-five minutes ahead of schedule, but Mr. Trammel and his assistant could be here any minute. We needed to get to work fast.

We went into the office, where I got started on the coffee while Ted booted up the computer. He'd made a terrific PowerPoint presentation last night to help sell Trammel on the idea of recovering the *Delia*.

"I should've brought cookies or muffins or something," I said. "I'll run down to MacKenzies' Mochas and get some." I looked at the clock and saw that it was nearly a quarter of nine. "Do you think I have time?"

"Yes," Ted said. "Just go. And stop stressing. I've never seen you this nervous before . . . and I've seen you in some fairly nerve-racking situations . . . way scarier than this."

"I know." I started to expound on why I was feeling nervous, but another glimpse at the clock reminded me I was running short on time.

I hurried down the street to MacKenzies' Mochas. Blake was working the counter, and I ordered a dozen cookies.

"Chocolate chip, peanut butter, oatmeal raisin— an assortment of whatever you've got on hand," I said.

"Where's the fire?" he asked with a grin. "And do you honestly believe you can put it out by throwing cookies at it?"

"Please, hurry," I said. "Some people are coming to the shop at nine for a meeting."

"Okay, okay." He got a brown-and-white-striped MacKenzies' Mochas box and filled it with cookies.

"Thanks, Blake." I placed enough money on the counter to cover the cost of the cookies and to give Blake a tip. "I'll tell you all about it later," I called over my shoulder.

When I got back to the Seven-Year Stitch, Ted was printing out the photos of the tapestry. I looked from the printer to Ted to the bulletin board. He'd removed the green felt and, other than a coupon for a half-price manicure and a photo of the Fabergé egg I was trying to re-create for Mom, the board was bare.

I set the box of cookies down by the coffeepot. "Where are the pictures I printed out yesterday?"

"I don't know. I remembered your saying last night that you'd pinned them to this board, but when I took the sheet of felt off, they were gone," he said. "I thought you might've taken them down and put them in a drawer or something. Anyway, it was quicker to reprint them than to wait and see where the others were."

"I don't know where the others are," I said. "The last time I saw them they were on that bulletin board covered by that piece of green felt."

"Do you think someone else might've come into your office without your noticing?"

"It's possible. I always leave the office door open during classes so the students can help themselves to coffee or water." I frowned. "But why would anyone want them? I was under the impression that not that many people knew about the tapestry."

"Not only would the person have to know that the tapestry existed—they'd have to know that Chester gave it to you for safekeeping," Ted said.

"Mary probably knew Chester gave me the tapestry. She'd left the house before he did so, but I imagine someone told her later," I said. "She came in here when she first arrived yesterday evening. She noticed the board, and I tried to blow it off as unimportant."

"Did she see the photos?"

I shook my head. "No, because I had the felt over it then. But curiosity could've gotten the best of her, and she could've come back in here and peeked to see what was beneath the felt." My eyes widened. "What if she did? What if she saw the photos and thinks I'm trying to take advantage of Chester's death by cashing in on his tapestry treasure map?"

Ted took me gently by the shoulders. "Did she confront you about it?"

"You know she didn't or else I'd know what became of the pictures. But she's a battered wife. Confrontation is probably not her strong suit."

"I wouldn't be too sure about that," he said. "Confronting her husband might not be her strong suit, but I imagine she'd at least ask you nicely about it, had she jumped to the conclusion that you were trying to make a fortune off Chester's tapestry."

"Who else could it be?" I wondered aloud.

"Did you actually look at the photos on the bulletin board before students began arriving and you started class?"

"No. The last time I looked at them was sometime yesterday afternoon," I said.

"Then it wasn't necessarily one of your students who took the pictures," he pointed out. "They could've been taken anytime from the moment you last saw them to the time we discovered they were missing. I'm going to say they were taken between yesterday afternoon and the time you closed up last night because there aren't any signs of forced entry."

Before I could respond to that, the bells over the door signaled the arrival of J. T. Trammel and his assistant. Mr. Trammel was as tall, broad, and Texan as I'd imagined him to be—even down to his bolo tie and caramel-colored Stetson hat. He was a bit older than I'd anticipated, and when he swept the Stetson off his head, I saw that he was bald.

"Howdy, there," he said. "You must be Marcy."

I held out my hand, and he grasped it in a firm shake. "It's so nice to meet you, Mr. Trammel. This is Ted Nash."

Ted and Mr. Trammel shook hands and exchanged pleasantries before Mr. Trammel introduced us to his assistant, Stacey.

Stacey, too, was older than I'd anticipated her to be. This thin, studious-looking woman in her early to midfifties looked more like a Madge or an Agnes to me. For some reason the Staceys I had known were always cheerleaders and prom queens. Those Staceys wore their hair in ponytails, not in slicked-back buns like *this* Stacey.

"Both of you need to get something straight right off," Mr. Trammel was saying, drawing me out of my reverie about his assistant. "You need to call me

J.T. Mr. Trammel was my daddy, and he's been dead nigh on to fifteen years." He cupped my chin and turned my face toward the light. "Yep, you sure look enough like Bev." He smiled at Ted. "She's a pretty little thing, isn't she? If we do this thing, we'll definitely have to get you on camera, Marcy. Make a note of that, Stacey."

Stacey apparently took this request seriously because she dutifully wrote something down on the steno pad she carried.

"Would you like some coffee and cookies before we get started?" I asked.

"Yeah, I'll have some coffee, please," J.T. said. "Two creams and four sugars."

"All right," I said. "Stacey?"

"Black, please." Her face softened, and she nearly smiled. I realized she'd be rather attractive if she did smile.

As J.T. and Stacey made themselves comfortable in the sit-and-stitch square, Ted unplugged the laptop—now that the battery was fully charged—and I prepared a tray with the coffee and cookies.

Since J.T. and Stacey were seated on the navy sofa facing away from the window, Ted and I took the club chairs. Ted opened the laptop and brought up the slide presentation while I handed J.T. and Stacey their coffees. I was too nervous to risk a cup yet—I was too afraid I'd spill it everywhere and on every-

one. Ted said he'd get a cup later. I pushed the tray a safe distance from the edge of the table and sat back in my chair.

"All right, then," J.T.'s big voice boomed. "Let's get down to brass tacks. Tell me why my network should invest in this project."

Ted pulled up the first slide. It was a painting of a ship—in fact, I think I'd noticed the painting hanging in the hallway in his apartment. "This is a schooner from the eighteen hundreds," he said. "The *Delia* was an East Coast schooner that sank off the coast of Tallulah Falls in 1844. The ship was en route to Portland from San Francisco and its cargo consisted of silk, beeswax, and pearls. The *Delia* was damaged during a storm and became stranded at sea. A tug eventually arrived in time to save the crew, but the schooner broke up and the cargo was lost."

"What makes you think there's anything left of this *Delia* to find on the ocean floor?" J.T. asked.

"You might recall that in 1985, the famous American treasure hunter Mel Fisher recovered a sizable treasure from the Spanish ship *Nuestra Señora de Atocha* that sank in 1622 off the Florida Keys," I said, feeling confident because *that* particular ship had sunk more than two hundred years prior to the *Delia* and there had still been treasure left to find.

"I did read about that," J.T. said. "And I remember the article saying that Fisher and his team searched for that wreck for more than sixteen years."

"True," I said. "But what a payoff! And in 2011, divers found additional artifacts from the ship."

"Yep, and it only took twenty-six more years." He waved his hand toward the laptop. "Keep going."

I decided then that my best bet was to hush and let Ted answer J.T.'s questions. Clearly, I wasn't helping our cause with my input.

The next slides showed the photos of the tapestry—the first one of the tapestry as a whole and then the smaller close-ups of various portions of the map. Ted explained that this was Chester Cantor's tapestry and that Chester believed it to be a map leading to the *Delia*. J.T. seemed skeptical, but he didn't say anything.

The next slide depicted spots all along the Oregon coast where ships had wrecked. Ted narrated, telling J.T. that the ships included the 1881 British ship *Fern Glen*, the first of four grain vessels to be lost within a month on the Columbia River; the mysterious brig *Blanco* that was found adrift in 1864 without a crew; and an American steamer called the *Brush*, carrying a cargo of lumber and merchandise from the Orient, that sank north of Cape Arago in 1923.

The final slide quoted text from Jim Gibbs's book *Peril at Sea*, which related accounts of divers finding gold ingots, Spanish coins, and other relics off the coast of Oregon.

J.T. gave an appreciative nod. "I'm guessing there are maritime museums and various historians we could interview about all these shipwrecks and alleged finds?" He was looking at me, so I felt compelled to answer.

"In addition to Tallulah Falls's historical society, there's the Tillamook County Museum," I said. "And we have the Columbia River Maritime Museum in Astoria, and there's the Coos Historical and Maritime Museum in North Bend. As for other historians, we have plenty of older people who love to talk."

I noticed Stacey was writing furiously in her steno pad.

"Tell me about this Chester Cantor," J.T. said. "What's his story?"

I glanced at Ted, and he gave me a slight shrug.

"Well, J.T., I guess Chester is a bit of a mystery himself," I said. "Chester told me that he believed he was a descendant of Jack or George Ramsay. Jack was reputed to have been the survivor of a mid-1700s shipwreck. Jack was of particular interest to the Clatsop Indians because he had red hair, fair skin, and freckles." I smiled. "They'd never seen anyone like him."

"In fact, the explorers Lewis and Clark mention a young man traveling with a party of Clatsop natives who had long red hair," Ted added. "This was in the early 1800s, so we're thinking this young man was the son of Jack Ramsay and a Clatsop woman."

"Who was George Ramsay?" J.T. asked.

"We think he was Jack's brother," I said. "Chester told me his great-grandmother's maiden name was Ramsay and that she was a redhead. That's one of the main reasons he put so much stock in her treasure map tapestry."

"I don't know if they're any relation because Peyton Ramsey spelled his last name R-a-m-s-e-y rather than a-y," Ted said, "but there's another Ramsey legend about a miner and his crew who struck gold near Oregon's Onion Mountain in the 1850s. The miners were attacked by Native Americans, and there were only four survivors. The survivors loaded their saddlebags with gold ore and tried to escape, but they were overtaken. They, too, where killed and thrown—with their saddlebags—into a nearby crevice."

"Was that gold ever recovered?" J.T. asked.

"Not that I'm aware of," Ted answered. "I read somewhere that in 1902 trappers found skeletal remains of some of the miners but didn't know to search for gold beneath the bones."

J.T. laughed. "That's a tough break. For them, anyway. It sounds as if Tallulah Falls has enough legends and stories and interesting people to make for some entertaining television—that's for sure. What about this Chester Cantor? Could we set up a meeting with him?"

"I'm afraid not," I said. "But I'd be happy to see if his son and daughter-in-law will talk with you."

"Why can't *he* talk with me?" J.T. asked.

I looked at Ted, hoping he'd supply the answer. He did . . . in his official detective voice.

"Chester Cantor was found murdered in his home on Friday afternoon," Ted said. "Although the Tallulah Falls Police Department is pursuing every lead, no suspect is in custody at this time."

J.T.'s eyes brightened and so did his smile. "A sunken treasure *and* a murder mystery? Now, that's what I'm talking about!" He stood, shook both our hands again, and placed his hat on his head. "I'll go call my people and get back in touch with you soon—probably before the day is out."

He breezed out the door with Stacey trailing in his wake and leaving Ted and me gaping and speechless.

Chapter Fourteen

When Ted left, he told me he'd run by my house at lunchtime and pick up Angus for me. Before I got busy, I called MacKenzies' Mochas and asked Sadie if she could come to the shop during a slow time.

"Marce, I just saw a stretch limo pulling out from in front of the Seven-Year Stitch," she said. "I'm not waiting for a slow time. I'll be right there."

The first thing Sadie noticed when she came in was that Angus wasn't there. "Where's the baby?" she asked.

"I left him at home this morning because I wasn't sure how my guests felt about dogs. I was afraid they might be allergic or something," I said. "Ted's going to bring him later, though."

She arched a brow. "Ted has a key to your house now?"

"Um . . . yeah. I had an extra made for when Mom visits, and Ted is using that one to get Angus."

"Oh. So tell me about these guests," she said.

"His name is J. T. Trammel, and he's considering Chester Cantor's tapestry and a recovery attempt of the *Delia*'s cargo as documentary fodder for a new television network."

"How exciting. I'm surprised the Cantors would agree to be a part of it, though."

"Why do you say that?" I asked.

"Well, people who live like the Cantors—in an abuser/victim relationship—try to keep their lives as private as possible," she said. "I studied that in either psychology or sociology or some other *ology* in college."

"You're right." I bit my lip. "I hadn't even thought of that."

"What aren't you telling me?" Sadie asked.

"It's more like what I haven't told the Cantors . . . Adam Cantor, I mean. I've spoken with Mary and she gave the go-ahead for me to put out some feelers, but Adam doesn't know anything about my idea. I'm *going* to tell him. I'm just . . . you know . . . waiting until the time is right . . . making sure Mr. Trammel wants to do the piece . . . that sort of thing."

She shook her head. "How do you get yourself into these predicaments?"

"It's not as difficult as you'd imagine," I said. "By

the way, did you notice anyone hanging around my office during class yesterday evening . . . maybe acting suspiciously?"

"Yeah, sure. There was the guy in the trench coat with the fedora pulled low on his brow who was standing near the door, asking people if they wanted a good deal on a watch. Or do you mean the cowboy with the six-shooters in each hand and a bandanna covering the lower half of his face? I think he was planning to hold up the stagecoach."

"Oh, ha-ha. You're so funny. I'll take that as a *no.*"

"Why would one of your students be behaving suspiciously?" she asked.

I explained about the photos that had gone missing from my bulletin board. "What concerns me most is that Mary saw them and now thinks I'm a dirty, backstabbing opportunist who's trying to profit from Chester's tapestry."

Sadie dismissed my concern with a wave of her hand. "Even if she had seen the photos and thought that of you—which I highly doubt—you'll set the record straight when you talk with her and Adam about the documentary. Don't worry about it."

"You're right."

She smiled. "Wouldn't it be incredible to have a film crew here in Tallulah Falls? I know you're used to being around that sort of stuff with your mom, but I think it would be so cool."

"Me, too," I said. "It could bring a lot of extra business to the town, especially to MacKenzies' Mochas and the Brew Crew."

"It would, wouldn't it? I hadn't even considered that bonus. I was only thinking about how neat it would be to see Tallulah Falls on TV."

"But, please, Sadie, keep this to yourself until I know something definite." When Sadie looked down at the floor, I added, "Of course, you can tell Blake, but he's absolutely the only one. And, for goodness' sake, don't tell him where Keira can overhear."

She raised her eyes to mine, a smile lighting up her face. "Thanks, Marce. Let me know when you hear something, all right?"

I told her I would, and she left. She was practically running when she passed the window on her way back to MacKenzies' Mochas because she could hardly wait to share the news with Blake.

There was a steady flow of customers that morning, but it wasn't until Vera Langhorne came in that I realized how badly I needed to let the Cantors in on my meeting with J. T. Trammel. I'd failed to anticipate the impact the sight of a limousine would have on a small town like Tallulah Falls.

"The whole town's abuzz with speculation about the limo that was sitting outside your shop this morning," Vera said as she came in and sat beside me on the navy sofa facing the window.

Not wanting to divulge too much information, I told a half-truth. "That was a friend of my mom's. He's a filmmaker."

She tilted her head, taking in my dress, shoes, and carefully applied makeup. "Is he considering you for a role?"

I laughed. "I hardly think so. I'd never met him, and I wanted to make a good impression." Time to change the subject. "I'll have to step up my stitching if I'm going to finish this Fabergé egg for Mom for Easter, don't you think?"

Vera looked at the cross-stitch project I held in my lap. "If anyone can do it, you can. It's starting to come together."

Ted arrived around noon with Angus. He also brought chef's salads for the two of us and a peanut-butter-filled chew toy for Angus.

"You're spoiling him, you know," I told Ted.

"Maybe a little."

"You're spoiling me too. I'm not used to having an actual lunch every day. I usually just have some crackers or baked chips and a soda."

He frowned. "I don't know how you do that. If I did, I'd have a killer headache by the middle of the afternoon."

"I probably will the next time I skimp on lunch

because you've gotten me used to having an actual meal," I said.

"Good." He smiled. "You need to be used to having a meal at lunchtime. That's why everyone sets an hour aside out of the workday."

"Some of us don't have an entire hour to spare out of the workday."

We sat down in my office and dug into our salads. Angus remained in the shop, content to amuse himself with licking the peanut butter out of his toy.

"J.T.'s limo apparently attracted a lot of attention this morning," I said.

"Tell me about it. Even Manu wanted to know what was going on."

"Vera asked me about it—well, she more or less asked when she told me the town was *abuzz* over the limo. I told her it was a filmmaker friend of Mom's."

"I told Manu the truth . . . in confidence," Ted said.

"What did he think?"

"He didn't say much other than to impress upon me—unnecessarily—the fact that you don't need to talk with the Cantors about this alone." He took a drink of his soda. "I don't want you to ever find yourself alone with Adam Cantor. If you do, call nine-one-one."

"Yet you don't believe he killed Chester."

"The man might not be a murderer, but we know he's abusive . . . and potentially dangerous."

"I know. Who *do* you think killed Chester?" I asked.

"I don't have a clue, sweetheart. I wish I did. We're still pursuing every lead, but they're drying up pretty fast."

I wiped my mouth on my napkin. "Here's something I don't understand. Chester had talked with Jack Powell about searching for the *Delia* wreckage, right?"

"That's what Powell says. Why?"

"Jack told me that Chester was paranoid and had refused to let him see the tapestry. But Ed, the guy we met at Captain Moe's, said that he'd seen the tapestry. What do you make of that?"

"Without having the whole story, I can't make much of it at all. Either Ed lied, or Chester *did* show him the tapestry but then something happened that made Chester regret it," Ted said. "Maybe Ed told other people about the tapestry and Chester's belief that it was a treasure map."

"Maybe so. You should talk with Ed to see where he was at the time of Chester's murder," I said.

"We did that on Monday," he said with a grin. "And we're currently following up on his alibi."

I blushed. "Sorry. I know I get carried away."

He smiled even wider. "I like it when you get carried away."

*   *   *

Later that afternoon, I was once again hard at work on Mom's Easter present. I was a little surprised she hadn't called yet to see how this morning's meeting had gone. Knowing Mom, though, she was probably more aware of what was going on at this point than I was.

A deliveryman brought a shipment of embroidery floss and yarn, so I had to set my work on the table and put the supplies away in the storeroom. While I was putting the yarns and flosses in their proper places, I heard someone come in. I could hear a somewhat familiar voice greeting Angus, but I couldn't put a face to the voice until I stepped out of the storeroom and saw Audrey Dayton.

Audrey was in uniform and had placed her hat on the counter. She was bent over petting Angus with both hands.

"What a sweet dog," she said when I entered the shop area. "What's his name?"

"Angus. Angus O'Ruff, to be precise."

"Cute." She laughed. "I was on my way to Mac-Kenzies' Mochas to get a coffee and thought I'd stop by and see how you're doing."

I invited her to sit down in the sit-and-stitch square. After we were seated, I confessed that I was beginning to regret getting so involved with the

Cantors. I told her about Mary's questioning me as to whether or not the police thought her husband killed his father.

"I had no idea what to tell her, other than to honestly say that I'm not privy to the police investigation."

"She should never have put you in that position," Audrey said. "I mean, even had you been a *witness* to the murder, she shouldn't be asking you about it. She needs to be talking with the police. And if she's honestly afraid that her husband is a killer, then she needs to get her daughter and get out of that house."

Angus had followed Audrey to the chair where she sat, and he dropped his tennis ball at her feet.

"Ah, you want to play now, huh?" She lobbed the ball into the shop, and Angus scrambled after it. "I've made it crystal clear to Mary on several occasions—and so have others, including Manu and Reggie—that we'll get her and Melanie out and protect them if she'll let us. Chester's death is merely another of Mary's reasons in a long line of excuses to stay with Adam."

"Do you know the Cantors well, then?" I asked.

"I wouldn't say that." Angus returned with the ball, and she threw it for him again. "I'm not sure anyone knows them well. In a household like that, there are more secrets than you can imagine."

She spoke as if by experience, but I knew it wasn't

proper for me to ask her about it. Instead, I told her about this morning's meeting.

"How should I approach the Cantors with this news?" I asked.

Angus came back and dropped the yellow tennis ball by Audrey's left foot. This time she ignored him. "Just pray the deal falls through."

"But why? This documentary could be a wonderful opportunity for them," I said.

Angus whined, but Audrey still paid no attention. "It could also be a nightmare. They'll have cameras shoved in their faces . . . their actions will be scrutinized. . . . That sort of thing is stressful for people living a happy life together. But for people like Adam and Mary Cantor . . . like Melanie . . ." She finally picked up the ball and rolled it toward the office. "Like I said, pray that the documentary doesn't happen. It'll be better for everyone involved . . . including you."

After Audrey had left, I reflected on the fact that Audrey and Sadie had said basically the same thing about the Cantors' reaction to the documentary. Still, I felt that Adam, Mary, and Melanie might benefit from the documentary. Even if the cameras *were* a bit intrusive, maybe seeing himself behaving like a jerk would be a wake-up call to Adam. Or, at least, knowing he and his family were being watched and filmed, Adam would be on his best behavior toward his wife and daughter, wouldn't he? Besides, how long would the camera crew be around? After all, it was a documentary, not a reality show.

That's what I honestly thought right up until the moment that J.T. called.

"Marcy," he said, "I've talked with the rest of the folks at Explore Nation. And after our conference call, they talked about it, and then they called other people and talked about it, and now I'm calling to let you know that they passed on the documentary."

For a moment, I was almost relieved. I wouldn't have to worry what effect the filming would have on the Cantors' already volatile home life. Granted, they wouldn't profit financially now, but they wouldn't realize they were missing out on something they never knew about . . . or, in Mary's case, hadn't really expected to come to fruition.

"They want to do this thing as a reality show," J.T. said.

Not sure I heard him correctly, I asked, "Excuse me?"

"You heard me, darlin'. We're thinking of calling it *Treasure Oregon*. What do you think?"

"I . . . um . . ."

"You see, we'll be investigating not only the *Delia*'s wreckage and, hopefully, salvageable booty but also the rest of the legends you and Ted presented us with." He gave a hoot of laughter. "We believe we've got at least enough fodder for a couple of seasons."

"But what if you don't find anything?" I asked.

"Aw, don't you worry about that," he said. "We'll find *something*, even if we have to bury it ourselves first. Now we want you to be our expert on tapestries. Look up everything you can about them: history, how they're made, that sort of thing. Also find out if any—other than this one—have been believed to contain treasure maps or any *Da Vinci Code*–type secrets, all right?"

"Okay."

"Also, can you give me the names of some locals who might be in the know?" he asked.

"There's a treasure hunter named Jack Powell who'd be interested in helping you," I said. "I know that Chester had spoken with him about helping him find the *Delia*, but neither had the money required to pursue it."

"Good. I'll want to talk with him. But most of all, I want to meet these Cantors. Set that up for me, will you, dear?"

I gulped. "Of course."

Chapter Fifteen

Remember those baked chips I mentioned to Ted earlier? Well, after talking with J. T. Trammel, I paced and ate about a blue million of those things. Then I sent Ted a text saying, *J.T. doesn't want to do a documentary. Instead, he wants to do a REALITY SHOW!*

After I sent that text, I paced a few more lengths of the office before sending him another text saying, *J.T. wants to meet with the Cantors ASAP. Should I cancel tonight's class?*

My phone rang. It was Ted. He probably wished I'd stop texting him every couple minutes. I should've sent him a text before he called asking him, *Do you want me to stop texting you? Please, reply A for yes or B for no.*

I answered the phone with, "Ted, I don't know what to do."

"Try to set up the meeting for after class," Ted said, with the calm authority of an excellent police detective. "Given Adam's reaction to me at his home Saturday evening—and the fact that his father's murder is an ongoing investigation—I shouldn't be there." He paused. "I'll send that young officer, Andrew Moore, to be there undercover in case there's any trouble. You can meet there at the Seven-Year Stitch. It's a nice, neutral place, and everyone involved knows where it's located."

"That makes sense."

"So that the limo doesn't attract too much attention this time, call J.T. and ask if Andrew can pick him and Stacey up at their hotel and bring them to the meeting," he continued. "If he asks why, tell him it's to free up parking space since there are several people coming. I'm afraid that telling J. T. Trammel not to arrive in a limo because it would draw too much attention would do about as much good as telling Lady Gaga to dress conservatively."

"I see your point. Who besides the Cantors should be there?" I asked.

"I'm going to ask Manu to see if Reggie can be there. As the sheriff's wife, maybe she can bring documentation informing J.T. of all the regulations and permits his team will need to have in place before filming begins."

I was impressed. "That's smart. I'd have never

thought of that." I knew Ted's real reason for having Reggie there would be to alert him and Manu to any signs that Adam Cantor was getting ready to throw a tantrum.

"I'm not really that concerned about regulations at the moment," Ted said. "I just think it would be wise to have Reggie on hand."

"You mean, if Adam Cantor gets out of control," I said.

"That, or anything else unexpected," he said. "Andrew will be undercover, but I'm hoping having the sheriff's wife in attendance will help keep Adam's temper in check. Plus, I think it would be a good idea for you to invite Jack Powell. For one thing, he can tell J.T. more about Chester's plan to search for the wreck."

"And for another, he can back up to Adam what Chester told me about the tapestry," I added. "Somehow, I doubt Chester shared much about the tapestry or anything else with Adam."

"I imagine you're right about that."

"What about that other treasure hunter guy Chester had spoken with . . . Ed?" I asked. "Should I ask him to come?"

"I don't think he's a good fit for this meeting. J.T. might want to talk with him sometime later on, but Ed didn't seem to believe Chester's contention that the tapestry was a treasure map."

"Is there anyone else you can think of that I should invite?" I asked.

"No, I think there will be enough excitement with the gang who'll be there as it is."

"Yeah, that's what worries me. I'll start with the Cantors and let you know what happens."

After talking with Ted, I had a plan of action. Instead of eating chips and pacing, I had calls to make. I started with Mary Cantor.

"Hi, Mary." I kept my voice upbeat and cheerful. Maybe if I didn't convey my anxiety about the meeting to Mary, she'd be okay with it. "Remember my asking your permission to get in touch with a producer about the tapestry and the *Delia* treasure?"

"Yes," she said. "Don't tell me someone was actually interested."

"Sorry. I'm going to *have* to tell you that. Not only is he interested—he'd like for you and Adam to come by the Seven-Year Stitch at seven o'clock this evening to meet him."

She was silent for several long seconds. "I didn't mention your call to Adam. I didn't dream anyone would take you seriously about the tapestry being a treasure map. I'm not sure how he'll take the news."

"I can break it to him, if you'd prefer. I'll tell him how this show could be the legacy Chester wanted to leave his family . . . how it could allow the family to do things they'd never have been able to do otherwise, you know, from a financial standpoint. . . ." I struggled to come up with other benefits.

"No," Mary said. "I need to be the one to talk with Adam. Then if he wants to come, we'll be there."

I thanked her and ended the call. Mary sounded nervous. I wondered if I should've been more adamant about being the one to speak with Adam. Of course, the prospect of being in the same room with both me and Adam could be the very thing that was making her nervous. After all, I knew about her secret plan to leave Adam and that the plan was thwarted only because the police officers sent to get Chester found him dead. Did Adam even know that Chester and I had spoken about the tapestry? Mary could be terrified that I'd inadvertently let something slip.

Mary called me back later on to let me know that she'd spoken with Adam and that they'd be attending the meeting. "Thank you, Mary. I'll let Mr. Trammel know."

"Fine. See you later." She still sounded kind of cool. But if she hadn't wanted me to pursue the documentary—which had now become a reality show—I wish she'd have said so when I'd spoken with her originally. I did let Mr. Trammel know immediately, and he agreed to let Andrew pick up him and Stacey at their hotel. I let Ted know *that*, and he was relieved. He was also glad I'd been able to talk the Cantors into coming so easily. After talking with Ted, I called Jack Powell who was thrilled to be included in the meeting.

Having made all my phone calls, I was back to being nervous. In fact, a part of me wanted to close up the shop, go home, and crawl into bed. The more rational side of me wanted to stick around and see what happened. Or maybe it was the rational side that wanted to go home and hide. The side that paced and ate baked chips was the one that eventually won out.

The class went well, despite the fact that I'd been so distracted by thoughts of the upcoming meeting prior to the students' arrival. Before class, I'd taken Angus home and fed him his dinner. Since I'd filled up on baked chips, I hadn't been hungry.

I cut class short by about fifteen minutes in order to get the students out before the people started arriving for the meeting. So that the students wouldn't feel shortchanged, I gave them coupons for twenty percent off any single item in the shop.

As soon as they left, I straightened up the sit-and-stitch square and made a fresh pot of decaffeinated coffee. Ted texted me and asked if I needed anything. I started to jokingly request that he bring me a tranquilizer gun, but I changed my mind and simply told him everything was good.

Reggie was the first to arrive. She gave me a warm hug and told me I looked nice. Her compliment made me glad I hadn't changed into something more casual, as I'd been tempted to do, while I'd been home with Angus.

Andrew, J.T., and Stacey were there soon after Reggie. I made the introductions and mentioned that there was fresh decaf in my office if anyone cared for a cup. No one took me up on the offer.

I'd met Andrew on previous occasions. He was young and right out of the academy. The lanky, green-eyed blond was a good officer—even though I felt he could be overly serious at times—and I felt he would quickly move up through the ranks. It spoke volumes that Ted had sent him to this meeting.

Reggie told J.T. she hoped J.T. didn't mind her attendance at tonight's meeting. "I find your work fascinating," she said. "And, naturally, I'm interested to hear about what your crew might be doing here in town. The fact of a show being filmed here could bring a lot of additional tourism our way."

J.T. smiled. "I'm honored you took time out of your evening to join us, Mrs. Singh. I also appreciate your bringing me the zoning requirements and permit documentation. Stacey will look it over, and we'll send it on to the powers that be."

Jack Powell was more than a little intimidated by J.T. when he first got to the meeting, but J.T. sensed that and was able to put Jack at ease. They were talking about Jack's past treasure hunting expeditions when, at last, Adam and Mary walked in. I had to restrain myself from breathing a sigh of relief. I had begun to worry that the Cantors wouldn't show.

I introduced Adam and Mary to J.T., Stacey, and Andrew, who I said was driving Mr. Trammel this evening. Upon telling them hello and that it was nice to meet them, Mary sat stiffly on one of the club chairs and didn't utter another word.

J.T. asked that the rest of us sit down. After we'd done so, he remained standing and began to explain what he and his film crew hoped to accomplish in Tallulah Falls and the rest of Oregon.

"I talked with Marcy this morning about a few of the stories that have been circulating about treasure in these parts for . . . gosh . . . centuries, I guess it has been," J.T. said.

Jack nodded his head in agreement.

"There's the legend about the ship named the *Delia*, whose cargo of a fortune in pearls and other Oriental treasures was never recovered," J.T. continued. "That's the one that initially captured my network's interest. But since talking with Marcy, I learned about other treasure . . . treasure buried by pirates and Sir Frances Drake . . . and even treasure that was thrown away—whether inadvertently or not—by Native Americans.

"My television network—a new network called Explore Nation that's set to launch next fall—is interested in doing a reality show touching on and searching for some of these treasures. We plan to call the show *Treasure Oregon*. As we run out of things in and around Tallulah Falls to explore, we can move on to other parts of the state. It could also spawn additional shows about treasure in other states. Are there any questions so far?"

"My wife said you were interested in some old tapestry my dad had. What does this have to do with that?" Adam asked.

J.T. smiled. "I understand that your father believed the tapestry to be a map leading to the location of the *Delia*."

"That's what Mary told me," Adam said. "But while he might've *believed* that, thinking something doesn't make it true."

"He *did* believe it," Jack said. "He believed it so much that he was trying to figure out a way to get the money we'd need to search for it."

"He never told me any of that," Adam said. "Heck, he never even told *me* about the tapestry. Wouldn't he have asked me to go in with him on finding this treasure had he thought it was legitimate?"

"Not if you were the one he wanted to find it for," Jack said quietly.

Adam opened his mouth to speak, but then closed it again. Then he leaned forward, placed his elbows on his knees, and lowered his head.

J.T. filled the awkward silence. "I'm going to have Marcy be our tapestry expert. I think the camera will love her." He winked in my direction. "She's going to give viewers an overview of how tapestries are made, give us a little background of their history and importance over the years, and . . . well, be eye candy." He chuckled. "I'd like to show the viewers your father's tapestry, Adam. And I'd also like to use it to attempt to pinpoint a location for the ship. Now, you don't need to worry that interlopers will see the map and get to the treasure before we do, because the majority of the season will be filmed before the first show even airs. What do you say?"

Adam raised his head. "I don't know. This sounds a little hokey to me."

"You could make quite a bit of money off this venture," J.T. said.

"I provide for my family just fine, Mr. Trammel," Adam said.

"I'm sure you do. But this could be extra. Wouldn't it be nice to take more luxurious vacations . . . to not have to save for your daughter's college education?" J.T. raised his arms. "Heck, wouldn't it be nice to see if your daddy's map pans out and we're able to find a treasure?"

"Yeah." Adam blew out a breath. "Yeah, I guess it would. Before I agree to anything, though, I want everything in writing. I want to see what I'm getting into before I sign off on it."

"Of course." J.T. turned to Jack. "I'd like you to be our treasure hunting expert, Jack. You've done this sort of thing for most of your life. And while we'll have people to shore up your efforts, you'll be one of the main stars of the show as far as this expedition is concerned. Will you do it?"

"Yes, sir!" Jack exclaimed.

"All right," J.T. said. "Am I forgetting anything? Stacey?"

"No, sir," Stacey said. "I think this covers everything for this group. Of course, we'll need to talk with the people at the historical societies and museums. I'll set that up for sometime next week."

"Good." J.T. turned back to address the rest of us as a whole. "Stacey and I are flying back to California tomorrow morning, but we'll be returning here the first of the week with a research panel, a film crew, and a dive team to get this project under way. Please, take one of our cards from Stacey in case you need to discuss anything further or have any questions before we get back to town."

Stacey closed her ever-present steno pad, put it into her briefcase, and drew out a silver business card holder. She gave each of us a card with Explore

Nation!, J. T. Trammel, and J.T.'s contact information.

Mary and Adam were the first to leave. Andrew, J.T., and Stacey were the next to go. Jack approached me en route to the door. He shook my hand so fervently that I was afraid he'd wring it off.

"Thank you so much for letting me be a part of this, Marcy," he said. "This show could be a shot in the arm to my treasure hunting career . . . and if not, who cares? I can retire and tell everybody I'm a television star!"

I laughed. "I'm glad you're excited about the show, Jack." I looked at Reggie to include her in my question. "How do you guys think Mary and Adam took the news?"

"Mary will take the news however Adam tells her to take it," Jack said. "As for Adam, I didn't get a good read on him. What about you, Mrs. Singh?"

"I felt that he was either touched that his dad wanted to do something as special as finding a treasure for him, or that he was upset that Chester hadn't included him in the plan," Reggie said.

I sighed. "I only hope that he doesn't get home and start thinking about the tapestry and change his mind."

Chapter Sixteen

I was more than ready to slip out of my dress and heels when I got home. I took a quick shower and then threw on a navy tracksuit and thick multi-striped socks. I was curled up on the sofa watching *Family Ties* on a retro TV station when Ted arrived.

"You look tired," I told him, as he slumped onto the sofa.

"You look comfy."

"I have another old sweat suit and plenty more socks upstairs," I said. "You're welcome to them."

He grinned. "I'm sure they'd fit really well." He removed his tie, jacket, and shoes before stretching out beside me. "I'm awfully glad that when you were furniture shopping, you bought this extra-large couch. How did the meeting go?"

I rested my head on his shoulder. "Andrew didn't give you a full report?"

"He did . . . but I'd like to hear your version."

I gave him a brief rundown of the meeting. "I'm not sure how Adam was feeling when he left the meeting. He seemed okay, but with that guy appearances can be particularly deceiving."

"It's not only Adam who Manu and I are worried about. If the person or persons who killed Chester Cantor did so to get the tapestry, then we—the police department—need to keep a watchful eye on you and the Cantors," Ted said. "The Cantors, because if Adam didn't kill Chester, the murderer might try to take the tapestry from them."

"But I gave you the tapestry."

"True, but we returned it to Mary Cantor," he said. "The tapestry wasn't at the crime scene, so there was no reason for us to keep it."

"And why do you feel you need to keep a more watchful eye on me?" I asked.

"Because you're my Inch-High Private Eye." His laughter rumbled in his chest, and he hugged me tighter.

"Secondary reason?"

He sighed. "You brought Trammel in to recover— or, at least, to attempt to recover—the *Delia's* cargo."

"So if the killer was after the tapestry and ultimately any treasure to be found, we've foiled his nefarious schemes," I said. "And that was part of my grand plan to draw out the killer all along."

"You're going to be the death of me," he said.

"Nonsense."

The episode of *Family Ties* that had been playing ended and another started. I sang along with the theme song: "What would we do, baby, without us?"

It was a sunny Thursday morning, so I had no qualms about leaving Angus in the backyard to play while I went to visit Riley at her law office. The office had always been immaculately and elegantly decorated. It still was, but now everything had a softer appearance than before. Or maybe it was merely my imagination. The floral brocade sofa remained centered on the Oriental rug and flanked by rose-colored wingback chairs, but a white angora throw now rested over one arm of the sofa. The large cherry coffee table was still so highly polished that everything else in the room was reflected in its surface, but instead of the designer floral arrangement that used to adorn the table, an abstract family sculpture held the role of centerpiece.

Even Riley's mom and administrative assistant, Camille Patrick, seemed softer somehow. She still wore her black-and-gray-streaked hair up, but it wasn't as severe a style as it had been before. And she was happier and more relaxed than I'd ever seen her.

"Marcy, how are you dear?" she asked.

"I'm fine, Mrs. Patrick. How are you?"

"I'm great." She chuckled. "I'm still getting used to the idea of being a grandmother, but it's growing on me rather quickly."

"Is Riley available?"

"She is, and it will do her good to see you. Her first appointment isn't for about an hour, so you two should be able to have a nice, long chat," Mrs. Patrick said. "Plus, Laura is awake, so you'll get to enjoy her too."

Mrs. Patrick came out from behind her desk and walked with me to Riley's office. She tapped on the door. "Darling, Marcy is here."

"Terrific! Come on in," Riley called.

Riley's office had changed quite a bit more than the lobby had since I'd seen it last. Though the office still carried over the rose and pastel blue color scheme of the lobby, extraneous furniture had been removed to accommodate a baby swing, a bouncy seat, a rocking chair, and a bassinette. Riley's desk, chair, file cabinet, and one guest chair were all that remained of her "office" furniture.

"I love what you've done with the place," I told Riley as she came around the side of her desk to give me a hug.

"Don't you, though? I take all my meetings in the conference room now."

"I'll leave you two alone so you can visit," Mrs. Patrick said, backing out of Riley's office. "If you need for me to come get Laura, just let me know."

"In her dreams," Riley said with a giggle as her mother closed the door. "She's nearly worn a path between her desk and the bassinette."

I peeped over into the bassinette where Laura was lying. She was cooing and kicking her legs. I was pleased to see that the blanket I'd embellished by embroidering her initials, a spray of flowers, and a butterfly in the corner was in the bassinette beside her.

"May I rock her?" I asked.

"Of course."

I picked up the baby and moved to the rocking chair near the window. "Oh, Riley, she's so gorgeous."

"*Merci beaucoup.* She takes after her mother." Riley winked.

"She does," I said. The baby had both parents' dark hair and eyes, but I could see that she would have the delicate facial features of her mother.

Riley sat back down. "It's good to get back into some semblance of a routine again. Now, if I could just drag myself to the gym."

She wore a plum pantsuit, and I could see that her figure was returning to normal even if Riley *hadn't* been to the gym. "You look beautiful," I said.

"You're sweet. I knew it would be like a fresh spring breeze for you to come by. So tell me what you've been up to," she said.

"There might be some excitement coming to Tallulah Falls."

Riley made a *pfft* noise. "I already know about your and Ted's romance, remember?"

The baby cooed, and it sounded almost like a giggle. Riley and I laughed.

"I'm not talking about Ted and me. I'm talking about reality television."

Riley made such a fierce grimace that I laughed again. Then I explained about yesterday's meeting with J. T. Trammel and the later meeting with Trammel, the Cantors, and Jack Powell.

Riley leaned forward when I told her about Jack's declaration to Adam that Chester was hoping to find the treasure for him. "What did Adam say to that?"

"Nothing. He just sat there looking down at the floor."

"What about Mary?" she asked. "Did she comment at all?"

"Other than saying it was nice to meet the people she was introduced to, Mary didn't make a sound the entire time they were there," I said. "It seemed weird to me. I mean, Mary acted kind of nervous when Reggie and I were at their house Friday morning before Adam left for work—and that was completely understandable, given the circumstances. But last night, she acted like she was some sort of robot or something."

"Maybe she and Adam had argued before they arrived at the shop," Riley said. "Or he might've told her 'When we get there, you sit down and keep your mouth shut,' and she was afraid to do otherwise. See if she acts more like herself at tonight's class."

"I will. You said you knew Adam from when your dad represented him on the assault charges, right?" I asked.

"That's right. Why?"

"Have you had much contact with Mary?"

"Not much. I saw her when she was in here with Adam a time or two but that's all." Riley frowned. "What are you getting at?"

"I just can't figure her out. I mean, would you let your daughter stay in a home with someone you thought might be guilty of murder . . . even if that someone was your husband?"

"Absolutely not," she said. "But for some women that decision isn't as easily made as it would be for you or me."

"I think Mary's friend Susan Willoughby is trying to convince her to leave."

"Susan Willoughby?" Riley scoffed. "Unless she's changed a whole heckuva lot since high school, the only reason that woman would encourage anyone to do anything was because she thought there was something in it for her. That woman's a snake."

"Really? I never would've guessed that," I said. "She's in the domestic abuse victims' embroidery class, so maybe she got out of whatever situation made her so bad."

"Whoa, whoa, whoa. Back up. Did you say Susan Willoughby is in the domestic abuse vics' class?"

"I did," I said. "But, please, don't repeat that to anyone. I'm not even supposed to reveal to most people that I'm helping with the class."

"Oh, pooh. You know I won't say anything," Riley said. "But do me a favor. Ask Susan ever so casually who was abusive to her."

"Okay." I drew the word out, not sure where Riley was going with this favor.

"If she says it was her ex-husband, Jared, I hope lightning strikes her on the spot."

"Riley!"

"I do," she said. "Because when we were in high school, Jared Willoughby treated Susan like she was a princess, and she treated him like dirt. She even got suspended once when one of the teachers saw Susan hit Jared with her baton."

"Then why did he stay with her?" I asked.

"Hello? Isn't that the same question you just asked me about Mary and Adam? The answers run the gamut from love to shame to fear to reasons only the person involved in the relationship can comprehend." She noticed that Laura had dozed off in my arms. "Here, let me get her." She stood, gently took the baby, and laid her in the bassinette.

"I'd like to talk with Jared Willoughby sometime," I mused softly. "I think it would be nice to meet him and form my own opinion of the man. Like you, Manu was amazed that Susan was in the class and adamant that Jared had never been abusive to her."

"Can you talk with Jared without being too obvious?" Riley asked.

"Sure."

"He's an auto mechanic. His shop is over on Fourth Street."

I smiled. "Come to think of it, the Jeep is due for an oil change."

I still had a little over an hour before I had to open up the shop, so I drove on over to Fourth Street. I knew it was customary to have an appointment for an oil change; but even if Jared Willoughby was unable to work me in, I could still maybe talk with him for a minute or two.

I parked the Jeep in front of the garage and went inside. "Hello!" I called when I didn't see anyone.

"Hello!"

The voice came from beneath a green sedan. As I

stepped closer to the voice, a fresh-faced young man with a smear of grease on his cheek rolled from beneath the car on a wheeled, vinyl-covered board that I later learned was called a car creeper.

"Can I help you with something?" he asked.

"I hope so. Are you Jared Willoughby?"

"I might be." His tone was teasing. "Who wants to know?"

"I'm Marcy Singer. I'm a friend of Riley Kendall's, and she tells me you're a very good mechanic."

"Well, she might've spoken a tad too highly of me," he said. "You know how those lawyers are. What are you driving, and what kind of problems are you having?"

"I drive a Jeep, and I'm not really having any problems with it," I said. "All it needs is an oil change."

"In that case, I can fix you up in about twenty to twenty-five minutes then."

"You mean, you can go ahead and do it now?" I asked. "I don't mind making an appointment and coming back when it's more convenient." I pointed toward the car he'd been working on. "I don't want to jump in line ahead of that person."

He gave a bark of laughter. "*That person* is my mom. She pays me by making me dinner and knitting me scarves, and she's constantly having me tinker with her car. And when I work on it, I drive it. So it's not going anywhere until I break for lunch. Besides, business is slow today."

"Then I'd sure like for you to change the oil in my Jeep."

"All right. Glad we got that settled. Pull her into this empty bay over here." He walked over to open the door to the bay while I went out to drive the Jeep around.

I drove the Jeep into the garage, got out, and handed Jared my keys. "Did you say your mom knits?"

"Constantly," he said. "In fact, I think she made an afghan or two for Riley's baby."

I took a business card from my wallet. "Would you mind giving this to your mom and asking her to stop by the shop and see me sometime?"

He read the card. "The Seven-Year Stitch—that sounds like her kind of place." He tucked the card into his shirt pocket.

"I have a Susan Willoughby in a candlewick embroidery class," I said.

His face hardened. "Susan's my ex-wife."

"I'm sorry to hear that . . . that she's your *ex*. I mean . . . rather than your wife. . . . She seems nice."

"Everybody seems nice until you get to know them. Remember that." He unlatched the hood of the Jeep. "You can wait in there." He nodded toward a small room that held a desk, a table, four metal chairs, a coffeepot, and a wall-mounted television.

"Okay," I said. "Again, I'm sorry."

He didn't reply, and I headed toward the tiny waiting area. I was really bummed that I'd made Jared Willoughby angry before learning anything very helpful from him. Not that there was anything particularly helpful that I *could* learn from him, but I felt like now I'd never know if there had been or not. But, at least, I was getting the oil changed in the Jeep. That's something I'd needed to do anyway.

I sat down on one of the cold metal chairs and watched a morning news show on the television mounted in the corner until my neck began to ache from the strain. Then I made do with listening to the program with an occasional glance at the TV whenever something caught my interest.

As promised, the Jeep was ready in just under half an hour. I still had time to run home and get Angus before opening the shop.

Jared Willoughby came in and made out a bill for me, and I paid him by check.

"Hey, I'm sorry I got touchy earlier," he said.

"It was my fault," I told him. "I hit on a sensitive subject."

He blew out a breath. "It shouldn't bother me after all this time. We've been divorced for over a year."

"Too bad hurt feelings don't come with expiration dates," I said. "Some wounds take a long time to heal."

"Sounds like you know what you're talking about."

"I do. When I first came to Tallulah Falls about six months ago, I was nursing a broken heart over a guy who'd dumped me a year earlier. He wanted me back not too long ago, and I'd grown so much since we'd been together that I wondered what I ever saw in him in the first place." I shrugged. "That revelation combined with finding someone far better for me . . . and *to* me . . . has made me a much happier person."

"I'm glad for you." He sounded sincere.

"Thank you," I said. "I hope that happens for you sooner rather than later."

He smiled ruefully. "That'd be nice. I cared for Susan for so long, I don't know what it would be like to have feelings for anyone else."

Chapter Seventeen

Angus and I got to the Seven-Year Stitch with five minutes to spare. I unlocked the door and flipped on the lights before rushing to the office to stow my purse and the tote bag containing the Fabergé egg cross-stitch project. I hung up my jacket and went back into the shop to ensure all the bins were adequately stocked.

My first customer came in about ten minutes later. After that, business was sporadic enough that I had plenty of time to work on Mom's Easter present. Sporadic business was often par for the course on sunny days. People preferred to be out enjoying the weather. They were more likely to come into the shop to stock up on supplies when it was cold and/or rainy, and they were preparing to settle in at home and work on their needlecrafts for a few days.

Angus picked up the toy Ted had brought him the

day before. The peanut butter was almost gone from inside it, but Angus still enjoyed chewing on the toy. He took it and stretched out by the window in the sunshine. I sat in the sit-and-stitch square and worked on Mom's Easter egg.

I was already imagining how I was going to embellish the egg after I'd completed the cross-stitch work. I was going to use a thin ribbon in a metallic silver to make a lattice pattern over the egg. Within each of the diamonds created by the lattice work, I'd put a small pink ribbon rose bud. I'd then decorate the lattice with clear beads and maybe small faux diamonds. I was eager to finish the cross-stitching so I could get to the embellishment phase of the project.

My cell phone rang. I was so concentrated on Mom that I expected it to be her calling. Instead it was Ted.

"Hey, sweetheart. I'm sorry, but I won't be able to come by for lunch today," he said.

"That's all right. You don't have to feel obligated to have lunch with me every day."

"I realize I don't *have* to, but it's become the highlight of my workday."

"Mine too," I said. "Angus and I will miss you."

Angus looked up from his toy chewing as if to acknowledge his agreement.

"May I buy you dinner before I go to class this evening?" I asked.

"Sure, that'd be great. Would you like for me to pick you up there at the shop or meet you at your place?" he asked.

"My place, please. I don't think there are many restaurants around here that would accommodate our furry friend."

"I know of only one," he said.

"Captain Moe's," we said in unison, sharing a laugh.

"But I think it would be best to keep a certain puppy to his established routine," I said.

"I guess you're right. 'Til then, Inch-High."

"'Til then . . . Tall-Dark."

Ted laughed. "That's new."

"Not my best effort," I said. "I'll have to work on it."

At around two o'clock that afternoon, I had a customer come in and buy ten skeins of lemon yellow yarn. I'd gone into the storeroom to get enough of the yarn to restock the bin when I heard someone come in the front door.

"Hi, there!" I called. "I'll be right with you!"

"Okay! This is a lovely dog you have!" a woman replied. Then in a falsetto to Angus, she said, "Yes, you are. You're a pretty dog. And, oh, what a sweetie pie you are!"

When I walked back out into the shop with the yarn, the customer was on her knees in front of Angus in the sit-and-stitch square with her arms wrapped around his neck. He was licking her ear.

"Oh, goodness," I said. "He'll get hair all over you. He's shedding like crazy right now."

"He's fine," she said. "A little dog hair isn't going to hurt me any."

"I do have a lint roller on the counter. You're more than welcome to use it," I said. "Let me restock this yarn, and I'll be right with you."

"That's a nice, bright color," the customer said, moving onto the sofa. She was a thin woman of average height—taller than I—and she had light gray hair that was cut to frame her face. She wore jeans and a green plaid shirt, and if I'd had to choose one adjective with which to describe her in the moment we'd met, I'd have said "sweet." The woman simply radiated kindness.

I restocked the yarn and returned to the sit-and-stitch square. "I'm Marcy, by the way. Welcome to the Seven-Year Stitch."

"It's a pleasure to meet you, Marcy. I'm Christine. I don't know how I've missed finding your shop before now. It's absolutely charming."

"Thank you. I'm glad you found us," I said. "And you are too, aren't you, Angus?"

Angus wagged his tail . . . which was what he was

doing even before I asked the question, but I reasoned that he wouldn't be wagging his tail if he wasn't glad.

"Angus," Christine said with a smile. "Did you have him with you when you got your oil changed this morning?"

"No. I left him at home. I'd gone to see Riley Kendall and her baby, and I don't think Riley is ready to introduce Laura to Angus yet." I frowned slightly. "How did you know . . . ? Are you Jared Willoughby's mom?"

"I sure am. He brought me your card when he came by for lunch today, and I told him, 'I have to get over there.'" She laughed. "I knew you must not have had Angus with you when you were at the garage or else Jared would've mentioned him. He did enjoy meeting you."

I drew my brows together. "If he truly did enjoy meeting me, then I'm surprised."

"He told me you asked about Susan," she said.

I nodded. "She's in a candlewick embroidery class I teach on Tuesday evenings."

It was Christine's turn to frown. "Susan is taking an embroidery class? That doesn't sound like the Susan *I* know. How is she doing in the class?"

"Well, the class has only met once." I grinned. "I'll keep you posted."

Christine still looked confused about her former

daughter-in-law enrolling in my class, so I added, "Maybe Susan is taking the class to support her friend, Mary Cantor."

She sat back against the sofa cushions. "That explains it." Like her son had done this morning, Christine's face hardened.

"You don't like Mary?" I asked.

"I don't even know Mary. I only know that once Susan met her and then set her cap for Mary's husband, she was done with Jared."

My jaw dropped.

Christine smiled wryly at my stunned expression, her face softening slightly. "I sort of doubt Mary knows the real reason for Susan's friendship with her either."

"Do you think Adam and Susan are having an affair?" I asked.

"I don't know."

"But Adam has the reputation of having a bad temper and . . ."

"Of mistreating his wife and daughter," Christine supplied.

"Well, yes," I said. "And Susan *knows* that."

"She doesn't care," Christine said. "Susan wants what Susan wants. The only thing that frightens me is that she'll give up on Adam and go running back to Jared . . . only to end up breaking his heart all over again."

"I hope she doesn't. He deserves so much better than that."

"I agree. He told me you'd been through a rough situation too and that you'd given him a pep talk," she said. "Thank you for that."

"You're welcome," I said. "Once he finds the right girl, all the pieces will fall into place. He'll realize Susan never really was the one for him."

"Well, between you, me, and Angus, I'm rather disappointed that you found your Mr. Right. You'd make me the perfect daughter-in-law: you love dogs, you have this cool shop where I could get a discount on all my knitting supplies, and you're easy to talk with."

I laughed. "You're easy to talk with yourself. And since your son was nice enough to work me in on the spur of the moment for my oil change, I'll give you the one-day pretend daughter-in-law discount pass of twenty percent off your entire purchase. How's that?"

"I should refuse your generous offer," Christine said, with a grin. "And I would, except for one thing."

"What's that?" I asked.

"For just today, I want to have a daughter-in-law who makes me proud . . . even if she is only pretend. I couldn't possibly pass that up."

When she said that, she nearly made me cry. What's more, I began to see Susan in an even more negative light than I had when I'd left Riley's office that morning.

Even on busy days there was generally a lull around three o'clock in the afternoon. I attributed this phenomenon to the fact that school was dismissed at around that time and that many of my patrons either picked up their children from school or made sure they were home when their children got there. Since I hadn't lived in Tallulah Falls a full year yet—I'd arrived here the previous fall—I hadn't been able to determine whether the three o'clock lull occurred during summer break or not. It would be interesting to see.

Regardless, I used today's break as an opportunity to call Mom.

"Congratulations, love," she told me. "J.T. called me last night and is psyched about this new project. I understand it's been upgraded from documentary to reality show."

"Yeah . . . how about that?"

"You don't sound terribly excited about this opportunity. J.T. tells me he's grooming you for a recurring role as an expert in all things textile and embroidery related. Think of what a boon that would be for the Seven-Year Stitch." She paused. "Is that it, darling? Are you nervous about appearing on-screen?"

"A little," I confessed.

"Don't let that stress you out. I'm already planning on doing your outfits myself. You'll look stunning. And then all you have to do is be yourself and let your personality shine through."

"I appreciate that you're willing to coordinate my costumes—I mean, outfits. I really do. It's just that I'm beginning to worry about the impact the show could have on our quaint town."

"That's nothing to be concerned about either," she said. "From what I've gathered from J.T., there's only so much ground that can be covered in Tallulah Falls. Then they'll spread out through the rest of the coastline and, eventually, the state. Trust me, they'll be intent on getting in, getting the footage they need, and getting on out."

"You don't expect the film crew to be too intrusive then?" I asked.

"Not at all. The reason reality shows are currently popular with television executives is because they're easily and cheaply made. And I'd say that within a couple months, they can get enough material to last for an entire season."

"I never thought of it that way."

"I know the show isn't the only thing on your mind, though," Mom said. "What else has you so pensive? Is it the Cantor murder?"

"That's a large part of what's bothering me, but a

new wrinkle has been added to that story just today."
I explained about Riley's animosity toward Susan, my
oil change at Susan's ex-husband's garage, and Jared's
mom's visit. "Riley and Jared's mom paint a very different picture of Susan Willoughby from the one I had.
Now I'm wondering if Susan is a whacked-out seductress or the devoted friend I'd imagined her to be."

"My money is on the whacked-out seductress,"
Mom said.

"You honestly think she'd leave Jared, who appeared to be a really nice guy who'd been devoted to
her, for *Adam*?" I asked. "Granted, Adam's good
looks might've turned her head momentarily. But
would she give up her loving home in the hope of
running off with an alleged wife beater?"

"In a heartbeat."

"Huh?" I asked, surprised by Mom's quick answer and matter-of-fact tone.

"Of course, she would. Darling, I work with ac-
tors, actresses, directors, producers, and screenwrit-
ers. This sort of drama is commonplace."

"There," I stressed. "In the world of Hollywood
and make-believe—not here . . . not in the real
world."

"The world is the same wherever you go," Mom
said. "You have people with high standards and val-
ues as well as people with low ones no matter where
you are."

"But it makes no sense. Susan would prefer to leave a man who adores her and wants to make her happy in order to chase after one who might not even want her?" I huffed. "Can you explain that to me?"

"Sure. Didn't you say Riley told you that Susan was mean to Jared when they were attending school together?" she asked.

I confirmed that's what Riley had said.

"That tells me she had no love or respect for the man even then," Mom said. "She was merely using him to either get out from under her parents' thumb or to bide her time while waiting for someone more exciting to come along . . . or both."

"I think a lot of us go for the 'bad boy with the heart of gold,' but wouldn't Susan think better of her choice once she realized Adam was abusive to his wife and daughter?" I asked.

"Not in the least," she said. "Susan has deluded herself into thinking that she's not the mouse Mary is and that Adam wouldn't treat *her* that way. Why, in her mind, he probably only treats Mary poorly because Mary deserves it. Or it's because Adam doesn't love Mary."

"You really should be writing your own screenplays, Mom. You have a knack for this."

She chuckled. "Maybe I should write a screenplay. Maybe I *shall* . . . when I retire from costuming." She paused. "Susan's duplicity—if true—certainly puts a new slant on Chester Cantor's murder, doesn't it?"

"I don't follow you," I said slowly.

"It opens up a whole new world of what-ifs. What if Susan and Adam were having an affair, and Chester found out about it? What if Chester confronted Adam or Susan or Mary with his findings? What if his death had nothing to do with the tapestry after all? What if he was killed so he wouldn't reveal someone's secret?"

Chapter Eighteen

Before leaving the shop for the day, I called Mac-Kenzies' Mochas and ordered two chicken salad croissants with chips and brownies. Although I'd planned on taking Ted out for a special dinner, I decided that could wait until this weekend. Today I wanted to be able to talk with him privately without the risk of being overheard.

I locked the shop door and hurried down the street to get our dinner before returning for Angus. I put the food in the front seat of the Jeep and then did another walk through the store before leaving. I was used to returning to the Seven-Year Stitch on Thursday evenings. Having class in the back room of the library threw me off slightly, and I double-checked to make sure I'd turned off the coffeepot, computer, printer, and lights before locking up for the night. Then I put Angus into the backseat of the Jeep, where a divider kept him from crawling into the front, and we drove home.

Ted pulled into the driveway just ahead of us. He got out of his car and opened the Jeep door for Angus while I got our food.

"I hope you don't mind," I said, holding up the MacKenzies' Mochas bag.

"I don't mind in the least," he said, as we went inside.

"I promise I'll treat you to a really special dinner this weekend," I said. "But I wanted us to be able to talk this evening."

"One, any dinner with you is special. And, two, I'm flattered that you wanted to keep me to yourself." He bent down and kissed me.

I put the MacKenzies' Mochas bag on the table in the entryway so I could fully enjoy that kiss. Naturally, we were forced to come up for air when Angus pressed his furry face between us.

"You sure know how to ruin a tender moment, don't you, buddy?" Ted joked. "I can see right now that we're going to have to find you a girlfriend."

"He's been f-i-x-e-d," I whispered.

"Good," he whispered back. "Then he and his wife won't have a bunch of p-u-p-p-i-e-s."

"What have you got against p-u-p-p-i-e-s?"

"N-o-t-h-i-n-g. The shelters are full of adorable ones that desperately need good homes," he said.

"Can we please stop spelling now? I had no idea Angus was so well educated."

I poked my tongue out at him. "Let's go eat."

We went into the kitchen, where I filled Angus's bowl with kibble while Ted got us some plates out of the cabinet. I loved that he already felt comfortable in my house. I stood on my tiptoes and kissed his cheek as I moved around him to wash my hands at the sink.

He took the food from the bag and gave some sort of male victory cry when he came to the brownies.

"I have ice cream and chocolate syrup to go with those," I said.

He picked me up off the floor in a crushing hug. "Where have you been all my life, woman of my dreams?"

"I've been right here," I said, laughing. "You must've had insomnia."

He loosened his grip so that I slid slowly down his body until my feet were back on the floor. "I'm serious about that. I'm glad I found you . . . glad I have you in my life."

I pulled his head down to mine, and we kissed until—you guessed it—we were poked by a cold, wet nose. Ted and I started laughing.

"What did you say, Angus?" he asked. "You said you need to go outside? Why, certainly, it would be my pleasure to open the door for you." He opened the door and Angus loped out onto the lawn.

I was still giggling as I took sodas from the refrigerator and set the ice cream out on the counter to soften enough to scoop. I opened the container of croissants and put them on our plates with the chips.

As we sat down at the table, Ted asked, "What's on your mind?"

"I've been rethinking Chester Cantor's murder," I said. "All along, I've believed it had something to do with the tapestry and the *Delia*'s unfound cargo. But now I'm wondering if it couldn't be something else entirely." I went on to tell Ted about my various conversations about Susan Willoughby throughout the day, ending with Mom's suggestion that Chester uncovered and confronted someone about a secret—such as, an affair.

"Our task force has considered that angle," he said. "There's no evidence that Adam was having an affair with Susan Willoughby or with anyone else."

"So you still think Chester was killed by someone who wanted the tapestry," I said.

"Not exactly. While we're continuing to explore all possibilities, the prevalent theory is that Adam discovered the plan to move Chester, Mary, and Melanie out of the Cantor home, flew into a rage, and accidentally killed Chester," he said.

"Something tells me you aren't sold on that theory."

"I'm not." He shook his head. "And it's not because there's compelling evidence to the contrary. It's nothing more than . . . a *gut feeling*. I can't really explain it."

This time when I arrived at the library for the domestic abuse victims' class and meeting, I pulled around to the back of the building and turned off my lights. As everyone driving themselves—rather than arriving in the deputy-driven van—had been instructed, I waited two full minutes before getting out of the Jeep. During the two minutes, I made sure no one had followed me and that no one was lurking at the perimeters of the parking lot. I got out, hurried to the door, and gave a sharp double tap.

"Good job," Audrey Dayton said when she let me in. "I saw you arrive on the surveillance camera monitor."

"Thanks." I patted my tote bag. "I brought the extra cross-stitch and needlepoint kits that were left over last week in case we have any newbies. Would you like to try one?"

"I might. I'll wait and see if there are any left after tonight's class."

I looked around the room. It was early, but she

and I were the only ones there. "I can hardly believe
I beat Reggie getting here."

"Yeah, she's usually the first here and the last to
leave," Audrey said.

I spread the extra kits out on the center of the table. "What does your boyfriend think of your having
such a dangerous job?"

She laughed. "Um . . . subtle much?"

I was too embarrassed to join in her laughter. "I'm
sorry."

"There's no need to apologize," she said. "There's
also no need to try to fix me up with anyone. That *is*
what you were getting at, isn't it?"

"It is. And I really should know better. I used to
hate for my friends to set me up," I admitted.

"Not a big deal. Just out of curiosity, though,
who'd you have in mind for me?"

"Todd Calloway. He owns the Brew Crew," I said.
"It's the pub and craft brewery directly across the
street from the Seven-Year Stitch."

"The Brew Crew, huh? I've never been there," she
said. "I'll have to check that place out."

Reggie arrived, saying she'd had to stop for gas.
"I hadn't realized how low the tank had gotten until
I was on my way here." She looked from Audrey to
me. "You two look like you're up to something. Am
I interrupting anything interesting?"

"I'm attempting to talk Audrey into trying her

hand at either cross-stitch or needlepoint," I said. "I think it would be an excellent way for her to unwind after a stressful day."

"And I don't believe I have the patience for it," Audrey said.

"I agree with Marcy," Reggie said. "You should give it a try. Begin one of these simple kits this evening, and if you don't enjoy it, I'll finish it for you."

"I'm on duty tonight," Audrey reminded Reggie. "I need to be alert and focused on my job."

"Then choose a kit and take it home with you," I said. "If you have any trouble getting started, stop by the shop tomorrow and I'll give you a hand with it."

"Fine. You two win." Audrey went to the table and chose a needlepoint horse's head. "I like this one. It reminds me of a horse my uncle had when I was a little girl."

After that, the students began filing in. Audrey resumed her post by the door, and Reggie and I sat down at opposite ends of the table and took out our own projects. By being on either end of the table, one of us would be handy to any student who might require assistance with her project.

The van arrived with the women from the shelter, and some of the other women who'd provided their own transportation started filtering in too. Unlike the previous week, Susan, Mary, and Melanie were among the last to get there.

"Here you are at last," Reggie said to them. "I was beginning to worry that you guys might've run out of gas like I almost did."

"No," said Melanie. "These two were being slow-pokes, as usual. Did you hear that we might be on TV, Ms. Singh?"

"I did!" Reggie exclaimed. "Congratulations. This could kick off an acting career for you."

"I know, right? Mom says for me not to get my hopes up. But my math teacher, Ms. Johnson, said, 'You don't know what you can do until you try.' She's always telling us to follow our dreams and stuff like that."

Melanie was beaming, and her smile was contagious to nearly all of the rest of us in the room. Only her mother and Susan Willoughby were unaffected by the young girl's excitement and optimism.

"Ms. Johnson sounds like a special teacher," said Audrey,

"She's the absolute best," Melanie said,

Once everyone had arrived, we worked on our embroidery projects while Reggie facilitated a discussion on legal rights. No one requested any embroidery help, so my mind wandered as I stitched. I could now understand what Audrey was talking about when she said she needed to remain alert and focused. The only thing I was focused on was the kitten I was stitching and the random thoughts flitting through my mind.

Was it possible that Adam and Susan *were* having an affair? The police had found no evidence of that. And although I'd only been around the two of them when they were together that Saturday night after Chester died, they didn't even appear to be aware of each other then. Of course, Adam had been grieving for his father . . . but wouldn't a mistress have at least hovered near him in case he should need her?

Besides the lack of any semblance of attraction between Susan and Adam, why would Susan go out of her way to befriend Mary if she was intent on stealing Mary's husband away? I definitely needed to talk with Susan to try to figure out what was in her head.

After class, I grabbed the first opportunity to speak with Susan alone. "Would you help me carry a couple things to my car?" I asked. I made the request quietly, afraid that someone else would volunteer.

"I need to get home," she said, avoiding eye contact with me.

"It won't take but a second," I said. "I actually just want to talk with you for a moment."

She still hedged.

"I met your mother-in-law today," I said.

That did it. She jerked her head toward the door. I tried to hand her a thin stack of the cross-stitch kits, but she ignored my outstretched hand so I simply dropped them into my tote bag with the needlepoint kits.

"*Former* mother-in-law," Susan said as soon as we got outside. "What did the old bag tell you about me?"

"Not much . . . only that she's afraid you'll go back to Jared and break his heart again."

She scoffed and began walking. "In his deluded dreams."

"Is he the reason you're here, Susan?" I asked. "Was he abusive to you?"

She shrugged. "I didn't have it as rough as some of these women have it."

"What about Mary? Did you have it as rough as her?"

"I'm not sure things are as bad as she wants everyone to think," Susan said. "By the way, have there been any new developments in Chester's murder case?"

"Not that I know of," I said. I cleared my throat. "Back to Mary, why don't you think she has it as badly as she lets on?"

"I don't know. Maybe she does. It could be that I merely haven't seen it."

"What do you think of Adam?" I asked.

She stopped walking. "What do you mean by that?"

"What's your opinion of him?" I stopped, too, and

turned to face her but it was too dark for me to be able to read her expression. "Do you think he could be reformed and be a better husband to Mary . . . a better dad to Melanie?"

"I've never known Adam to mistreat Mel." She resumed walking toward the parking lot. "He's strict, sure, but he isn't mean to her."

"You think there's hope for the family then." I phrased this as a statement rather than a question.

"For him and Mary? I doubt it," she said.

"Why's that?"

"Because I don't think Mary loves him anymore." She ducked her head and hurried to her car, a silver Toyota that had seen better days. I'd thought maybe she, Mary, and Melanie had ridden together, but it was apparent that she was alone.

I got into the Jeep and followed Susan out of the parking lot. It was merely coincidence that we were going in the same direction to begin with, and I had no intention of tailing her to see where she was going. . . . I guess it would be more accurate to say that I had no *conscious* intention of following her to her next destination because that's precisely what I did.

Susan drove all the way to Depoe Bay to Captain Moe's. I pulled the Jeep into an empty space in the back and watched her walk into the diner. She kept looking to her left, her right, and behind her as she made her way from the car to the door. I didn't know if that was because she'd been aware that I was behind her and she was looking for me, or if it was because she was looking for someone else.

I had the feeling she was meeting someone. I waited a full five minutes after Susan had gone inside to see if Adam Cantor showed up. He didn't, but he could've arrived ahead of her and been waiting for her inside.

I got my purse and went into Captain Moe's. He was busy when I first walked through the door, so that gave me time to scan the dining room. I spotted Susan in a corner booth. But it wasn't Adam Cantor she was with. It was that guy Ed, who had interrupted Captain Moe when he was talking with Ted and me the last time we were here.

Captain Moe finished with his other customers and came over to greet me with a hug. "What a pleasure to see you back so soon! Where's Ted tonight?"

"He couldn't make it," I said.

"Table for one then? Or would you prefer a stool at the counter?"

"Can you spare a few minutes to talk privately?" As I asked the question, Susan glanced up. When she saw me, her eyes initially widened and then narrowed to slits.

"For you, always," Captain Moe said. He stepped to the counter and asked his manager to handle things for a little while, and then he directed me through the kitchen to his office.

As you might imagine, Captain Moe's office was very nautical. There was even an eight-spoke ship wheel on the wall behind his desk. Instead of sitting at his desk, however, he ushered me over to the sofa on the other side of the room.

"What's on your mind, Tinkerbell?" he asked.

"I sort of followed Susan Willoughby here," I said.

He shook with suppressed laughter. "How do you sort of follow someone?"

"Well, you follow them, but then you feel badly about it because it was kind of a creepy thing to do," I explained.

"I see. Why are you sort of following Susan Willoughby?"

I took a deep breath and told Captain Moe about my new theory that Susan might have been or be having an affair with Adam Cantor. "My theory is that if Chester found out and confronted them, then Adam might've lashed out at Chester and . . . you know . . . accidentally killed him."

"Sorry, Tink, but I believe you're barking up the wrong tree with this one. Susan comes in here fairly often, but she's always meeting Ed Harding."

"He's the guy she's sitting with right now, isn't he?" I asked.

Captain Moe nodded. "That's the one. Don't ask me what she sees in him, though."

"What can you tell me about him? Have you known him long?"

"No, I don't know that anyone here in Depoe Bay has known him long. He only showed up here about eight months ago," he said.

"I've only been here that long, and you know me."

"Ah, but you're easy to know. That one tends to keep to himself." He stroked his beard. "I'm not particularly keen on the man. . . . I get a bad vibe from him. He's rude—as you and Ted saw the other night—and he doesn't seem to do much."

"You mean he's lazy?"

"I get the impression that he either can't or doesn't want to hold a job. He's in here all hours of the day and night, which is contrary to someone who has a schedule to keep," he said. "Oh, and he never pays. If Susan isn't with him, he requests that his meal be charged to her. Then the next time they're in here together, she pays it."

"Are you kidding me?" I asked.

He smiled. "Not this time, Tinkerbell."

Chapter Nineteen

When I came out of Captain Moe's office, Susan and Ed were gone. Captain Moe walked me out to the parking lot, afraid that the couple might "waylay" me if Susan was indeed certain I'd followed her here. Thankfully, we didn't see them. Nor did I see Susan's car. I got into the Jeep, waved goodbye to Captain Moe, and went to Ted's apartment.

I knocked on the door, and while I waited for Ted to answer, I thought I should probably have called first to let him know I was stopping by. He answered the door fresh from a shower with a wet head, bare feet, and dressed only in fleece lounge pants. When he saw that it was me, he removed the safety chain from the door to allow me to come in.

"This is a pleasant surprise," he said, placing the nine millimeter handgun he held in his right hand onto the table by the door.

"I'm glad it isn't an *un*pleasant one."

He laughed as he closed and locked the door. "Given my line of work, I can't be too careful." He pulled me to him, and I ran my hands up his muscular arms to his shoulders.

"My goodness . . . you"—my mouth suddenly went dry—"you sure do take excellent care of yourself."

He chuckled—a deep, rich sound that sent goose bumps down my spine. "Thank you. I like the way you look too." He lowered his mouth to mine, and I was glad Angus wasn't here to interrupt us this time.

I eventually came out of my Ted-induced stupor and remembered what I'd stopped by to tell him. "You'll never guess who Susan Willoughby met at Captain Moe's tonight after the domestic abuse victims' support group meeting."

"Adam Cantor?" he asked.

"No. That would be the obvious answer," I said. "It was Ed Harding, that weird guy who interrupted when we were talking with Captain Moe last Saturday evening."

"I remember Ed. We had him brought into the station, and he provided one of our officers with an alibi for the time of Chester's death," he said.

"Did the alibi hold up?"

He waffled his hand. "It could neither be confirmed nor denied. He said he was at the library, but no one recalled seeing him at the time of the murder."

"But he was seen there before and after the time of the murder, right?"

"You got it, Inch-High. But what motive would Ed Harding have for murdering Chester?" Ted asked. "He'd seen the tapestry, and he didn't buy Chester's claim that it was a treasure map."

"Or that's what he wanted us to think," I said.

"If he'd believed Chester, then why didn't he simply agree to help him? Why did Chester have to turn to Jack Powell to enlist his aid in the treasure hunt?"

"I don't know." I sighed. "Jack did say Chester wouldn't show him the map. He said Chester was paranoid. We've already speculated that Chester's paranoia could've been because of something Ed did. What if Ed attempted to get Chester to give him the map? Or what if he tried to steal the map, and Chester caught him?"

"If that was the case, wouldn't Ed have killed Chester then?"

"I guess I'm grasping at straws, huh? It was so strange to see that Susan was having some sort of clandestine meeting with Ed Harding that I thought there had to be more to the story than a lurid affair."

"And how'd both Susan and you come to be at Captain Moe's after the meeting?" Ted's lips were twisted into a wry grin that told me he was already pretty sure he knew the answer to that question.

"I might've tailed her . . . a little."

"You know, that could be considered harassment or stalking or some other crime for which I'd have to lock you up and throw away the key," he teased.

"Oh, really?"

"Uh-huh." He spread his hands. "I could possibly be persuaded to look the other way this one time if you offered the proper leverage."

"Then, by all means, let me see if I can persuade you."

Friday morning, I went to the library to talk with Reggie. She was manning the front desk when I went inside.

"Hey, there," she said. "We're shorthanded today, so I'm helping out up here. What brings you by?"

I looked around to make sure there was no one standing near enough to overhear us. "Last night after class, Susan Willoughby drove to Captain Moe's and met with Ed Harding."

Reggie wrinkled her brow. "And?"

"Well, don't you think that's odd? She was meeting with someone who also had a connection to Chester Cantor."

"In a community the size of Tallulah Falls, that's not uncommon," she said. "*I* had a connection to Chester . . . as did you, Audrey, Jack Powell, and I'm sure many other people."

"But, Reggie, Chester showed Ed the tapestry. And Ed's alibi for the time of Chester's murder is that he was here," I said. "That can't be verified, but it can't be disputed either unless someone saw him outside the library during the time in question."

A patron came in and put a stack of books on the desk.

"Thank you," Reggie said. She turned back to me. "I'm not sure how to help you with this one." She looked back at the patron, a tiny older woman with a crooked spine, who'd returned to ask a question about a current bestseller.

"Just tell me what you think of Ed . . . you know, the author we were discussing," I said.

To the patron, Reggie said, "I'll see if the book is currently in the library or if it's checked out." She typed some data into the computer and waited for a response. "Personally, I don't care for that particular author," she told me. "I think he's sloppy and unfocused. That doesn't make him a *bad* author . . . I just don't like his stuff." She smiled at the patron. "Ms. Beasley, that book is out but is due back on Tuesday. Shall I reserve it for you?"

The patron confirmed that she would like the book reserved before tottering away from the desk.

"I can see how busy you are," I told Reggie. "I'll talk with you later."

I went home for Angus, and we went on to the

Seven-Year Stitch. We were earlier than usual, but I knew I could make good use of the time dusting, going over my inventory, and taking out the trash. I started with the least attractive chore—the trash.

I gathered the garbage from the small bins in the shop, the office, and the bathroom and placed it all into a large bag. Leaving Angus in the shop, I slipped out the back to put my bag into the Dumpster in the alley behind the store.

I was nearly to the Dumpster when I felt someone's arm snake around my neck. The person had a strong hold on me, and I was unable to turn my head to see who it was. I was beginning to feel lightheaded. Fearing I'd never survive the assault without a fight, I brought my heel up into my assailant's shin while simultaneously driving my elbow into his sternum. When he'd loosened his grip just enough, I went limp and tried to drop to the ground. My hope was to get out of this person's clutches and then get up and run. Instead, he caught me sufficiently to turn my fall into a push. I lurched forward, hitting my head on the Dumpster.

The next thing I knew, I was floating . . . and my head hurt like the dickens. I tried to open my eyes. It took too much effort. But the floating feeling was beginning to bother me. Since when could I float? I tried again and succeeded in opening my eyes. And I saw Blake . . . specifically, his chin. I noticed there was a tiny patch of hair on it that he'd missed when he'd shaved that morning.

"Chin," I mumbled.

"Be still until I get you in here to the sofa," he said.

I realized I wasn't floating after all . . . which was good because if I had been floating, I was probably dead. Blake was carrying me. "You've got me," I said to him.

"That's right, sweetie. I've got you."

"My trash . . . did I get it put into the bin?"

"I'll take care of it later." He placed me gently onto the sofa and leaned close to my face.

There was that patch of hair again. I raised my index finger and placed it squarely on that hairy patch and said, "Not by the hair of your chinny, chin, chin. Get it?"

I thought that was a funny joke. Blake apparently did not. Instead of laughing, he dabbed a tissue to my head.

"Ow!" I slapped his hand and began crying. Despite how loud my weeping sounded in my own ears, I could hear Angus whining.

"Shoo," Blake said. "Not now, Angus."

"Let him see me. Y-you're mean." I sobbed harder. "Are you the one who pushed me?"

"Sadie, help." Blake was talking on his phone. Angus came to my side and licked my face.

"Something's happened to Marcy and we have to get her to the hospital," Blake said. He put his phone in his pocket and put his face close to mine again. "Here. Let me see your eyes."

"Did you push me?" I asked again.

"You know I'd never hurt you." He was staring into my eyes—actually from one to the other—and I believed him. And I was sorry I doubted him.

"I'm sorry. I know you wouldn't hurt me." My eyes drifted shut.

"Marcy . . . Marcy, stay with me, babe." His voice was coming from far away. "Come on. Look at me. Is that what happened? Did someone attack you?"

"It's okay. I know . . . you didn't. . . ." I was so sleepy. I just wanted him to be quiet and let me sleep.

"Sadie, thank God you're here," Blake said. "I don't know . . ."

That's all I heard. I was vaguely aware of people trying to wake me up. I mean, there were a bunch of voices. I later learned that in addition to Sadie and Blake, Todd, Ted, and Manu had arrived after Sadie had called them.

Ted and Manu took me to the hospital, with Ted in the backseat with me talking, soothing, and trying to keep me conscious. They told me that during my periods of lucidity—and they used that word loosely—

I was concerned with two things: whether or not my bag of garbage had been left in the alley instead of placed into the Dumpster where it belonged, and why nobody else seemed to think it was funny that Blake had missed a spot while he was shaving.

Todd took Angus over to the Brew Crew, and Sadie locked up the Seven-Year Stitch before returning to MacKenzies' Mochas to mind the coffee shop while Blake followed us to the hospital. Since Blake had been the first to arrive on the scene, they knew the doctors would want to talk with him.

Fortunately, my injuries were all concentrated above the neck, and I was able to remain clothed during my examination because all three men stayed in the room with me once we got to the emergency room. A nurse bandaged the cut on my head and recorded my vital signs. Not long afterward, the doctor came in. I wondered if the hospital staff was normally this efficient or if my being escorted by the Tallulah Falls Police Department's sheriff and head detective had factored into my speedy treatment.

"Did you lose consciousness at any time?" asked the ER physician, a youngish man with curly black hair and a full beard.

"No," I answered. "I don't think so."

"She was unconscious when I found her," Blake said. "And then she drifted in and out."

"Can you—any of you . . . all of you—tell me

what happened?" The doctor shone a tiny light into my eyes. "Let's begin with you, Ms. Singer, and then someone else can fill in any blanks you might have."

"I got to work early and decided to do some housecleaning," I said. "I always take out the shop's garbage on Friday because the sanitation truck comes by first thing Saturday morning."

"All right, Ms. Singer," he said. "And what were you doing immediately prior to your accident?"

"I was taking the garbage out." I was sleepy. Maybe if I could tell this guy what he wanted to know, he'd let me go home and take a nap. I closed my eyes and tried my best to remember. "I went out the back door and into the alley with my trash bag. Someone must've been waiting on me because he grabbed me in a choke hold."

"Did you see who it was?" Manu asked.

I shook my head. "We fought, and he pushed me." I opened my eyes. "That's all I remember."

The physician turned to Blake. "You said you found Ms. Singer?"

"Yes. I always park behind the building. When I arrived this morning, I saw Marcy lying against the Dumpster."

"What time was that?" the doctor asked.

"About nine thirty," Blake said.

"And, Ms. Singer, what time did you take out the garbage?"

"Probably around nine fifteen . . . something like that."

"Blake, did you see anyone leaving the crime scene?" Manu asked.

The doctor shot Manu a look of exasperation.

"Sorry, but I didn't notice anything except Marcy lying there on the pavement," Blake answered Manu. "It scared me half to death."

I looked at Ted. His face was drained of color and appeared to be as hard as stone. "Please, take me home," I said to him.

"I will, sweetheart," he said, "as soon as the doctor says it's okay."

The doctor did some neurological tests and reported that I could go home. He said that someone would need to stay with me and monitor my condition for the next twenty-four hours and that it was fine for me to sleep—joy!—as long as my caregiver woke me every two or three hours for the first twelve hours. I guessed that was to make sure I hadn't died in my sleep. He told them to bring me back if I experienced any of a laundry list of problems that I didn't feel like listening to and tuned out.

Ted volunteered to stay with me, and Manu said he'd take us by Ted's apartment so Ted could get a few things to take to my house.

"Reggie and I will bring your car over to Marcy's place later this afternoon," Manu said.

"And Sadie and I can get the Jeep home," Blake said.

"What about Angus?" I asked.

"We'll get him home too." Blake squeezed my hand. "You just worry about getting better."

"What's to get better?" I asked with a weak smile. "You know I have a hard head."

All three men nodded in agreement that I was a hardhead, but I was too tired to pretend to argue with them.

When we got to Ted's apartment, I stayed in the car with Manu while Ted went in to pack an overnight bag.

"Ted isn't saying much," I told Manu.

"The more upset he is, the quieter he becomes. He'll be all right when he realizes you're going to be okay," Manu said. "We're going to find whoever did this, Marcy."

"Do you think it was a random act, or that someone targeted me specifically?" I asked.

"We'll investigate both possibilities. Which do you think it was?"

"Right now, it feels pretty personal," I said.

Chapter Twenty

Manu dropped Ted and me off at my house and said he and Reggie would be back to see us later. When we got inside, Ted and I went into the living room. I eased onto the sofa, and I realized again what a comfortable piece of furniture it was.

"Do you need something to eat? Something to drink?" Ted asked.

"I'm fine." I patted the cushion. "Sit with me."

"I will in a second. I'm going to run upstairs and get you a pillow and—"

"I don't need a pillow," I interrupted. "All I need right now is you."

He sat with me then and gathered me into his arms. "I was scared when we got the call from Sadie telling us you'd been hurt. Nobody knew what or how bad your injuries were, and they couldn't really tell us what had happened to you. The only thing we knew for sure was that Blake had found you in the alleyway and that you'd hit your head."

"See? It wasn't as big a deal as you'd thought it was."

"It's big enough . . . and I'm not about to leave you unprotected until we find whoever did this."

"Do you think it was random?" I asked.

"I don't know. If so, it's quite a coincidence that it occurred the morning after you followed Susan Willoughby to Depoe Bay," he said. "I'm afraid it could also be connected to Chester Cantor's murder."

"That's what I'm afraid of too. It could've been Adam . . . Ed. . . . Heck, it could've even been Susan. I didn't see the person at all."

Ted kissed my temple—the one without the big bandage over it. "Try not to worry about it. Manu is out there right now tracking every lead, and I won't let anything else happen to you."

The doorbell rang, and Ted was on instant alert. He got up, peered through the window, and recognized Todd's truck. Still, he called, "Is that you, Calloway?" Upon Todd's confirmation, Ted opened the door.

Angus hesitated only a moment in front of Ted. Then he spotted me in the living room and came racing toward me. The two men shared a look of fear that the big, gangly dog would leap onto my lap and hurt me, but I had no such qualms. I knew my dog . . . and he knew me. He realized something was wrong.

When he got to the sofa, he sat on the floor in front of me, placed his head on my knee, and whined softly.

"It's okay, baby," I said, gently stroking his ears. "I'm okay."

Ted and Todd joined Angus and me in the living room.

"How're you feeling?" Todd asked.

"My head still hurts, but I'll be fine," I said. "Thank you for taking care of Angus."

"Anytime. I'd better be getting back to the Brew Crew. If you need anything, let me know." He nodded at Ted. "You take care of her."

"I will. Thanks." Ted walked Todd to the door, and I heard Todd tell him to "find who did this." Ted assured him that he would.

Before Ted could finish seeing Todd out, Vera Langhorne arrived.

"Hello, dear," she said to Ted. "Where's our patient? Oh, never mind; I see her." She sailed into the living room, the white cape she wore billowing around her and reminding me of a sail. "You poor darling! I heard you were the victim of an attempted mugging." She perched beside me on the sofa. "Let me see your face." After examining my wound, she said she didn't think there would be scarring. That was a possibility I hadn't even considered. Vera pulled me to her heavily perfumed side in a one-armed hug. "I'm so glad you're all right. You could've been killed!"

"I don't think it was as serious as all that," I said, sitting back up before Vera's perfume made me sneeze. I was afraid a sneeze might make my head explode, given the way it was aching.

"Ted, would you, please, be a darling and go out to my car and bring in the gift bag on the passenger seat?" Vera asked. "In my excitement, I forgot it." When Ted hesitated, she said, "I'll be right here by her side."

As soon as he walked out the front door, Vera hugged me again and said, "See how he cares for you? It's absolutely precious."

I didn't respond. After all, what could I say? *Actually, he's afraid to leave because there might be a killer after me.* That would make our visit awkward in a hurry.

Ted returned and handed Vera the bag.

"Thank you, Ted." She then passed the bag to me. "This isn't anything much, dear, just a couple things that I hope will make you more comfy as you heal."

I dug through the layers of various colors of tissue paper to find a pair of light blue silk pajamas and a small box of Godiva truffles. Vera had superb taste. I told her so and thanked her profusely.

"You're quite welcome," she said. "Is there anything else you need?"

"Nope. I'm good. But thanks anyway," I said.

She looked from me to Ted and back again. "I suppose you really do have everything you need." She winked. "By the way, all the merchants in the square are being extra-vigilant—some of them are looking out for themselves, of course—but if they see anyone loitering about, they're going to call the police right away."

"Thank you," Ted said.

"I won't keep the two of you any longer, and I can see myself out." Vera hugged Angus, gave me one more quick squeeze, and then breezed out.

Ted reclaimed his place beside me on the sofa. "I hope there aren't any more visitors for a while. You need some rest."

No sooner had he uttered those words than the doorbell rang. I laughed and then winced at the pain.

"After this one, I'm taking you upstairs to bed," he said.

I raised my brows.

"To rest." He answered the door. Instead of a visitor, it was a delivery.

Riley Kendall had sent a bouquet of yellow and white roses, a small box, and a note. The note said: *Get well soon, Marce. The box is from Uncle Moe, and I have no idea what's in it.*

I opened the box. Inside were two DVDs—*Hook* and *Finding Neverland*. He, too, had included a note: *These are to aid your recuperation. Dinner for you and the detective is on me as soon as you're up to it.*—CM

"How sweet," I said, with a smile. "I'm touched by everyone's thoughtfulness."

"So am I. But you really do need to get some rest. Let's get you upstairs."

"No, let's stay here and watch one of these movies," I said. "Surely things will settle down now." I held up the box of truffles. "We have snacks."

He grinned. "You've talked me into it."

Ted made us popcorn to accompany the truffles, and we watched *Finding Neverland*. After the movie, I dozed off.

I'm not sure how long I slept, but when I awoke, Ted had covered me with a blanket and was sitting on the chair across from me with his legs stretched out on the ottoman. He was using his e-reader, and the light from the device was the only one in the room.

"Hi," I said.

He got up, came over to me, and bent down to check my eyes. "Who am I?"

I smiled. "You're the man of my dreams."

"I'm serious," he said.

"So am I." I huffed. "Fine. You're Ted Nash, and I'm Marcy Singer."

"Who starred in the movie we watched earlier?"

"Johnny Depp and Kate Winslet," I answered.

"How's your head?" he asked.

I started to sit up.

"Not too fast." He helped me into a more upright position and sat beside me so I could lean against him.

"My headache has eased," I said. I gingerly raised my hand to the bandage on my forehead near the temple. "This place still hurts." I recalled Vera's mention of scarring. "It *will* heal up and go away . . . won't it?"

"No one will remember it was ever there."

"If it does leave a scar, I'm sure Mom knows someone who can fix it," I said.

"Should we call and let her know what happened?" Ted asked.

"Not yet. I don't want to worry her . . . especially when whoever did this is still out there."

Sadie and Blake came and brought the Jeep to me. They also brought a goodie basket filled with my MacKenzies' Mochas favorites. As soon as they walked into the living room, Blake strode over to the sofa and showed me that he'd gone back and shaved again and that his entire face was smooth.

"I'm sorry," I said, unable to stifle a giggle. "I have no idea why I fixated on that."

"Here I am thinking you're at the threshold to death's door, and you start poking me in the face and quoting from that piece of classic literature, 'The Three Little Pigs,'" he continued.

We were all laughing so hard that we didn't hear the doorbell ring. In fact, we wouldn't have known anyone was there if Angus hadn't gone and barked at the door.

Ted went to see who was there and returned with a large white box bearing a red velvet ribbon. "More gifts for Her Majesty."

"I'm the hero here," Blake said. "And did I get any presents today? Say it with me, people: 'Not by the hair of my chinny, chin, chin!'"

"You can have this one," I said. "Go ahead. Open it up, Blake."

"Is this a trick? Do you already know what this is?" he asked. "Is it something you ordered?"

"No," I said.

He looked at Sadie. "What do you think, babe? What usually comes in a box like this one?"

"Let me think," Sadie said, a smile playing about her lips. "Boxes like that generally contain superhero outfits, naughty underwear, sexy thigh-high boots . . . um . . . what else, Marce?"

"I don't know," I said. "That's a comprehensive list there."

"Well, I would enjoy any of those things," Blake said. "They would make me feel attractive and undo some of the hurt I've suffered today over being compared to a trio of swine."

Referencing the movie *Babe*, Ted said, "That'll do, pig. That'll do."

This brought about another fit of laughter. Finally, I wiped the tears from my face and told Blake to open the box already before he caused my headache to return.

"No way." He handed me the box. "I'm not opening your present."

"Come on," I said. "I want to see your face when you take the lid off my thigh-high red leather boots."

"Red? I imagined they'd be black," Blake said. "I don't even want them now."

"Sorry. Red goes with my Wonder Woman costume." I opened the box, and boy, did that wipe the smile off my face. Inside was a wreath. And so I wouldn't get the wrong impression and think it was a decorative wreath meant to adorn my front door or something, it had a sash across it with the words REST IN PEACE.

"What is it?" Ted asked, stepping closer to me. He muttered a curse when he saw what was in the box.

I noticed a yellow slip of paper like that from a

legal pad. Written on it was: *You're trying to destroy Tallulah Falls. I'm trying to destroy you. Next time, I'll do a better job.*

"This is not one of my favorite deliveries," I said, trying to keep my tone light. "It's not even in the top ten . . . unless I was doing a list of *worst* gifts."

Sadie moved over beside me and placed her arm around my shoulders.

Ted was already on the phone to Manu asking him to get crime scene techs to the house on the double. He was also asking him to check out Blooming Occasions to see if it was a legitimate floral service.

When Ted ended the call, he took the box to the kitchen.

"I've never heard of Blooming Occasions," Sadie said when Ted returned to the living room. "Have any of you?"

"Not me," I said. "But I'm still discovering new places."

"I haven't heard of it," Blake said. "And I've been in the doghouse enough times that I know every florist in this county."

Sadie rolled her eyes.

"I haven't heard of it either," Ted admitted. "But Marcy has been receiving things all day. The van had a Blooming Occasions logo on the door, so I didn't think anything of it."

"The van could've been stolen," I said. "Or the

logo could have been one of those magnetic signs you can get made up at a print shop."

Blake gazed around at our downcast expressions. "What are you guys looking like sad sacks for? I'm the one who got screwed out of my thigh-high boots."

It was a good try, but the mood had been spoiled.

Chapter Twenty-one

There were no apparent leads as to who sent the wreath. No floral vans had been reported stolen. None of the printers within a twenty-five mile radius recalled doing any work for Blooming Occasions. The only logical conclusion was that the suspect made the magnets himself and put them on a van he either owned or had borrowed.

No fingerprints were found on the box, the ribbon, the wreath, or the note except for mine and Ted's. Ted's were only on the box. He'd been careful not to touch anything else. Even the delivery person, who'd not yet been located, had worn gloves.

We were all frustrated: Reggie because she blamed herself for the attack since she attributed it to my involvement with the Cantors; Manu because he couldn't uncover a single lead in the attack; Ted because he feared for my safety; and me because I wanted to put all the drama behind me and go back to work tomorrow.

"It's too risky," Manu said. "The doctor said you needed to be under observation for twenty-four hours. Besides, I don't want you at the shop alone."

"But Saturday is one of my best days," I said. I turned my gaze on Ted.

"Had today not gone as it did, I was planning on staying in the office as much as possible tomorrow and catching up on some reports I need to file," he said. "I could do those on my laptop at the Seven-Year Stitch as easily as I could at the station."

"All right, then," Manu said. "I'll keep you posted on whatever I can find. I'm not giving up until this guy has been caught."

"Are you scheduled to work Sunday, Ted?" Reggie asked.

"I am, but I've got plenty of vacation days built up."

"Nonsense," she said. "Go on and work. I can hang out with Marcy on Sunday." She looked at me. "That is, if you don't mind."

"I don't mind at all," I said.

"Thanks, Reggie," Ted said. "If there aren't any changes in Marcy's condition, I might take you up on your offer."

After they left, I told Ted I didn't like having a babysitter. "So what if you need to work Sunday?

I'll be fine. The doctor *did* say twenty-four hours, not forty-eight, right?"

"He did say twenty-four, sweetheart, but I think it's going to take a little longer than that to soothe Reggie's conscience."

"But she has nothing to feel guilty over."

"Put yourself in her place," he said. "You get your friend involved in a situation in which one person is murdered, a woman and a child are living in a potentially dangerous home, and your friend has just been savagely attacked."

"I see your point." I smiled and extended my arms to him. "Besides, not *all* babysitting is bad."

On Saturday morning, I wore a jaunty red beret to cover the bandage on my head. To make it work, I also wore a long-sleeved black ballet-neck top, black cigarette pants, and red flats. Ted told me I looked like either a Bohemian poet or a Parisian artist.

"Why do I have to be a *Parisian* artist?" I asked. "Can't I be a Tallulah Falls artist? Can't I paint you *ici* in the Seven-Year Stitch?"

"Of course. I'd be flattered," he said, sitting on the sofa in his non-Bohemian attire of jeans and a blue sweatshirt. "I wasn't aware that you were a painter."

"*Mais oui.* I paint very well. What color would you like to be?"

He gestured toward the laptop he'd just turned on. "Should I put this back up and take you to the ER?"

I strode over to the sofa, took Ted's face in my hands, and pressed my nose to his. "Look at my pupils."

He chuckled. "Your pupils are okay. It's your mind I'm concerned about."

I kissed him and then twirled away. "It's the beret. It does something to me . . . makes me sassy." I giggled. "Besides, yesterday was such a downer. I want us to have fun today."

"Not all of yesterday was a downer. Parts of it were fun."

"True, but I want *all* of today to be fun." I winked at him over my shoulder and went to check on our coffee.

"Whew!" Ted called, laughter evident in his voice. "I don't know whether or not I can handle you in beret mode . . . but I'm sure going to enjoy trying!"

When customers started coming in, Ted had to move to the office so he could concentrate on his paperwork. Whenever I could catch the shop empty for a few minutes, I'd go into the office and work on a report on tapestries I was preparing for J. T. Trammel.

I found that there were a lot of Old World–type maps depicted in antique tapestries. These tapestries often had the two hemispheres depicted in various shades of tan, brown, and bronze. Some tapestries narrowed their focus to more specific geographic locations, and others were woven into breathtaking works of art having nothing to do with maps whatsoever.

I learned that tapestry designers must make a detailed pattern called a *mise en carte*, and then they transcribe the colors and contours prior to weaving. To imagine someone doing all that and then hand-weaving a treasure map for her children—or her children's children . . . or whomever Chester Cantor's great-grandmother had hoped to empower with the tapestry—was simply mind-boggling.

The bells over the door jingled, and I jumped up to hurry into the shop.

"Careful, *ma petite* Inch-High," Ted said softly.

I was grinning when I left the office, but that grin froze on my face when I saw Adam Cantor standing just inside the door petting Angus.

"Hi, Mr. Cantor," I said.

The clatter behind me attested to how quickly Ted had come up out of his chair.

"Hello, Marcy." His eyes widened. "And Detective Nash . . . Sorry. I didn't see you there at first."

"Hi, Adam," Ted said. "What brings you by?"

"I heard about the accident and wanted to drop in to see how Marcy is doing," he said. "So . . . how are you?"

"I'm fine, thanks," I said, now recovered enough from my surprise to take advantage of the opportunity to talk with Adam Cantor. "Would you like to sit and visit with us for a few minutes?"

"Sure."

The three of us moved to the sit-and-stitch square, where Ted and I sat on the sofa facing the window and Adam sat on the club chair to our right.

"I couldn't help but notice that during the meeting with J. T. Trammel the other night, you appeared startled to learn that your father wanted to find the treasure of the *Delia* for you," I said.

Adam blinked in surprise, and Ted squeezed my hand slightly. I didn't turn toward Ted because I knew he'd be wearing his formidable why'd-you-do-that detective face.

Adam cleared his throat and scratched his head, but when I continued to stare at him expectantly, he said, "It was a shock. I mean, I knew Pop had an old tapestry somewhere that had been passed down to him . . . and I'd heard him tell Melanie stories about treasure and sailing the ocean and what the two of them could do with the fortune they'd discover. . . . It was fairy-tale stuff. I never dreamed there could be any truth to any of it. I wasn't even aware that he knew the location of the tapestry after all these years."

"There's something I want—need—to explain to

you," I said. "When we went to see your father that Friday morning with the books . . ."

Ted pressed my hand again, so I slid it out of his grasp.

"I know what I'm doing," I told him. "Trust me. Mr. Cantor needs to hear this." I returned my focus to Adam. "As we talked, your dad found out I had this embroidery specialty shop and correctly assumed that I'd be interested in seeing his antique tapestry. He showed it to me and explained its history and *his* history. He was proud of his ancestry."

Adam smiled. "And heaven knows Pop liked to talk."

"Mr. Cantor, I don't know why your father would trust me with the secrets of his tapestry, but he did," I said. "And he told me that he wanted to find this treasure so that you—his family—could have a better life. That's why I told Mr. Trammel about the tapestry. I wanted your dad to get his wish."

"But there's no guarantee there even is a treasure to be found," Adam said.

"True, but the network doesn't care," Ted said.

"Exactly. And by sharing your family's tapestry and allowing the film crew to use it to search for the *Delia*, you'll be well compensated," I said. "I'm guessing Mr. Trammel will be bringing contracts when he returns on Monday."

"Have an attorney look yours over and dicker

with Mr. Trammel if you don't feel he's offering enough," Ted said.

"Your dad was a dreamer," I told him. "I think Melanie is too. She's excited about the possibility of appearing on TV. But, being more practical, this could wind up being your dad's way of paying for his granddaughter's college education. Wouldn't that be cool?"

"How did you know Melanie is excited about the film crew coming to Tallulah Falls?" Adam asked.

Ooops. I got too cocky. Think fast, Marcy! "I ran into her at the library the other day."

He nodded. "I should go. I've got some errands to finish up, and then I might go home and have Mary iron that old tapestry."

"Oh, please, don't," I said. "The tapestry is really delicate and should only be ironed or cleaned by a professional."

He smiled. "Right. Well, anyway, you guys have made me feel better about Explore Nation. Glad you're okay, Marcy."

He left, and I shot Ted a triumphant smirk. "See how unnecessary all that squeezing turned out to be?"

"First off, he nearly tripped you up when he asked about Melanie."

"Was it that obvious?" I asked.

"It was to me. Hopefully, it wasn't to Adam. That's one of the reasons squeezing you was absolutely necessary. I had no idea what you were about to say," he said. "Even on a good day, I'm not sure anyone—including you—knows what you're going to say before it leaves your brain and tumbles out of your mouth. Today you had two additional strikes against you."

"I'll concede yesterday's head injury," I said. "What's the other strike?"

"The power of the beret. I feared it would lead you astray."

"That's so Seussian," I said, with a laugh.

"Actually, I thought it sounded like the beginning of a limerick," he said. "But, seriously, job well done. I'm proud of the way you handled the conversation with Adam. The next time the department needs an arbiter, I'm recommending you."

"It wasn't a big deal. I just wanted him to know why I pursued the treasure hunt with the network," I said. "I didn't want to gain anything by it . . . and it's not my intention to destroy Tallulah Falls."

"Do you think Adam sent the wreath? That he's the one who attacked you?"

"I don't know." I took Ted's hand. It was warm and strong and comforting when it wasn't squeezing me to try to keep my mouth shut. "Adam is a relatively big man. He could've hurt me badly, had he been the one who attacked me. I get the impression that this person was smaller than Adam Cantor."

"Do you believe it could have been a woman?" he asked.

"It's possible . . . but it was important to me to let Adam know at least part of Chester's hope for his family," I said. "It might not do any good, but I know now that I've done everything I can to help."

Ted kissed me. "You're one special woman."

A pair of customers came in—sisters who often visited the shop together on Saturdays to see if I had anything new—and Ted returned to the office.

Angus spent most of the day lying by the window with his chew toy that Ted had refilled with peanut butter. When he had to go out, Ted insisted that we go together. He said the fresh air would do us all good. I knew he didn't want me to be alone.

Mom once told me, "Let your man be your hero . . . even if the only heroic thing you have him do is open a pickle jar. It'll make you both happy."

She was right, as usual. And so was Ted. It *did* do us all good to stroll down the street. He and I held hands, and Angus loped along in front of us. And it was especially nice that one time when Ted cleaned up after Angus. The fact that it made him gag was the proverbial icing.

We were headed back to the Seven-Year Stitch, and I was poking fun at Ted when two engines of the

Tallulah Falls Fire Department went tearing down the street. I froze.

Ted, ever adept at reading my thoughts, said, "It's not your house, sweetheart. They're going in the wrong direction."

When we got back to the shop, Ted washed his hands and then called Manu to find out what was going on.

"It's the Cantors," he told me. "Their house is on fire."

I gasped. "Is it bad? Was anyone hurt?"

"All Manu knows at this time is that a call went out requesting dispatch to send fire trucks to the Cantors' address," Ted said. "He recognized the address because he's seen it so much recently because of Chester's death."

"That poor family. We should go over there."

"Marcy, we need to stay here and let the fire department do its job." He placed his hands on my shoulders. "I feel badly for the Cantors too, but right now we'd just be in the way."

"Manu said the call requested fire trucks but not ambulances, didn't he?"

"That's what he said."

I leaned into Ted, and he encircled me in his arms. "I hope everyone's all right."

"I wonder if the tapestry was destroyed."

"Ted, how can you think of the tapestry at a time like this?" I asked.

"The note you received yesterday with the wreath said you were destroying Tallulah Falls," he said. "The only thing you've done that would affect Tallulah Falls in the least is the fostering of the reality show, and you did that with the tapestry."

"So you think the fire might've been set on purpose in order to destroy the tapestry and stop the production of the reality show," I said.

"And stop the search for the *Delia*." He reached into his pocket and took out his phone again. "Manu Singh," he said into the phone.

When Manu answered, Ted told him his theory.

"Given the fact that Chester was murdered," Ted told me after he'd ended the call, "Manu had already placed a team of officers and an arson specialist on the scene. He'll let me know as soon as he has further information."

I shuddered, and Ted hugged me again.

"Let's get you and Angus home," he said.

I was more than happy to comply with that suggestion.

Chapter Twenty-two

Ted and I were in the kitchen making pizzas when Manu and Reggie came by. They sat at the table while we finished adding cheese, onion, pepperoni, and sausage to one pizza, and cheese, ham, and pineapple to the other. Ted popped both into the oven, and then we sat down with Manu and Reggie.

"Will you join us for dinner?" I asked. "I've already tossed the salad, and it's in the refrigerator. The pizzas should be done in ten to fifteen minutes."

"Thank you for the offer, but we stopped at Mac-Kenzies' Mochas on the way over," Manu said. "I missed lunch today and then was at the Cantors' place all afternoon. I was ravenous."

It was obvious the day had taken a toll on Manu. His deep-set brown eyes were bloodshot, and there were dark circles beneath them.

"What caused the fire?" Ted asked.

"Was anyone hurt?" I asked.

Since Ted and I had spoken at the same time, Manu answered my question first. "No one was hurt. There wasn't anyone home at the time of the fire. That's the good news." He lifted his eyes to Ted's. "Here's the bad—it was arson. The firefighters told me that the odor of gasoline was overpowering and that it was concentrated in the small back bedroom."

"Chester's room?" I asked.

Manu nodded. "That's right."

"Was most of the damage concentrated there then?" Ted asked.

"Nothing in that room survived the blaze, but the fire spread quickly," Manu said. "The family lost pretty much everything."

"That's horrible," I said. "Poor Melanie. She's lost her grandfather and her home in just over a week. I mean, my heart goes out to Adam and Mary too, but all this must be particularly devastating to Melanie." I looked at Reggie. "What can we do?"

"Ted, are you working tomorrow?" Reggie asked.

"Unless Marcy needs me here, I'll be at work," he answered. "I want to help investigate this fire. And I also intend to dig a little deeper into the Cantors' personal lives to see whether the fire was set in order to destroy the tapestry or whether the treasure map is merely a red herring that someone is using to throw us off the real reason the Cantors are being victimized."

"All right, then perhaps Marcy and I can take a care package over to the hotel where the Cantors are staying," Reggie said. "I don't know what we can come up with, and it probably won't be a lot, but it will show them that their community cares."

The oven timer dinged, and I got up and took our pizzas out and placed them on wire racks to cool.

"That's a good idea," I told Reggie. "And I know all of Tallulah Falls will come together and lend a hand as soon as word gets around."

Reggie smiled. "In this town, word has more than likely already gotten around . . . twice."

Manu stood. "We'll go now and let you enjoy your dinner. See you tomorrow."

After another attempt to persuade them to stay and eat, we walked Reggie and Manu to the door. Reggie had been disappointed she hadn't gotten to see Angus since he'd been in the backyard during their visit, so she went to the fence and patted his head.

Ted winked at me when he heard Manu pleading with his wife to "Come on . . . I'm tired. . . . You can play with him tomorrow."

"I wonder why they don't have pets of their own," I said. "Reggie is obviously an animal lover."

"Manu loves them too, but he's allergic," Ted said.

"Oh, my gosh, I had no idea."

He grinned. "Stick with me, kid. You'll learn a lot."

After dinner, I called J. T. Trammel. I thought it was only fair to let him know that the tapestry had more than likely been destroyed in the fire. Stacey answered J.T.'s private number, and it finally penetrated my thick skull that she was more to him than his assistant.

"Hey, Marcy, what do you know?" J.T. asked when he came on the line.

"I have some bad news," I said.

"Well, don't beat around the bush. Let's have it."

"The Cantors' home was set on fire today. It was almost a total loss, and it's probable that the tapestry was destroyed," I told him.

"You say the fire was *set*?" he asked.

"Yes, sir. It was definitely arson."

"Marcy Singer, you beautiful little doll!" He laughed. "If you were standing here right this minute, I'd kiss you!"

"But won't this ruin your plans for the reality show?" I asked.

"Are you kidding? You still have the digital photos of the tapestry, and reality television doesn't get any better than this. Before we've even started filming, we've got us a murder and a house fire," he said. "We can speculate that other treasure hunters are sabotaging us . . . or that the treasure is cursed. Our ratings will go through the roof! Thanks for the update, darlin'. See you on Monday."

I ended the call and then stared at the phone in stunned silence.

"What is it?" Ted asked. "Was he more upset than you'd expected him to be?"

"Upset? No." I tried to emulate J.T.'s voice. "He's delighted . . . thrilled out of his cotton-picking gourd. If I wasn't sure he was in California, I'd think he kindled that fire himself."

Ted slipped his arm around me. "Maybe he was drunk or something and doesn't understand the ramifications of the fire."

"Oh, he understood all right," I said glumly. "He told me that reality TV doesn't get any better than this, that ratings would be great, and that if I was there he'd kiss me. Trust me. He understood perfectly."

"I suppose if you take away the human element—put aside the impact of this fire on the family who lived in the home—you do have danger and excitement. Television programs cash in on people's misfortunes all the time," he said. "I guess J. T. Trammel is just looking at the bottom line."

"I'm beginning to wish I'd never even heard of Explore Nation . . . that I'd kept my nose out of the Cantors' business," I said.

Ted stifled a laugh. "A leopard can't wish his spots away."

"Is that right?" I picked up a pillow. "Well, then, maybe you can *beat* them off of him!" I slung the pillow at Ted's head.

I got in a couple of good licks, but looking back on it, I'd have to say the pillow fight ended in a tie.

I was working on Mom's Fabergé egg when Reggie arrived the next morning. I was making good progress and was almost two-thirds of the way finished with the cross-stitching. Reggie bragged on the egg and then, as Manu had known she would, she played fetch with Angus.

"So what's our plan for today?" I asked.

"After I got home last night, I called some of our local merchants and explained what had happened to the Cantors," she said. "Most of them had already heard, of course, and all were eager to help. Some are donating merchandise, others are giving gift cards or cash, and a few are even doing both."

"That's fantastic," I said. "I love how our town comes together in a crisis. Even though I didn't suffer much of a crisis on Friday, the gifts and cards and phone calls from my friends meant a lot to me."

"Yes, for the most part, Tallulah Falls is a wonderful town. There are just those few bad apples that hurt us all."

"Speaking of bad apples, do you think the same person who attacked me is the one who set fire to the Cantors' home?" I asked.

"I believe it's a strong possibility," she said. "Why?"

"Because I think it's a strong possibility too, and that's why I've decided to stay here with Angus today. If someone burned my house down with Angus in it, I'd never forgive myself."

"I understand completely. I'll call the merchants and reschedule my pickups until after Ted gets off work."

"Please, don't do that," I said. "The Cantors need you today. I'll be fine."

"Are you sure?"

"Positive."

"Okay. I'll come back here as soon as I've made the delivery," Reggie said.

I smiled. "If you'll call me before you leave the hotel, I'll make us some lunch. In the meantime, maybe I can get this egg finished."

About half an hour after Reggie left to visit the Cantors, Angus decided he needed to visit the backyard.

I got up and let him out, and then I fixed myself a cup of tea. I stood at the window, watching him play with a Kodiak bear chew toy—he'd toss it up, run and get it, and then heave it into the air again. Suddenly, he stopped playing and ran to the fence. He jumped up and draped his lanky front paws over the top and started barking. I couldn't see who our visitor was yet, but it was certain that we had company.

As I placed my teacup on the counter and headed for the entryway, the doorbell rang. I looked through the narrow glass to see Susan Willoughby. She wasn't my favorite person—especially since meeting and talking with Jared and his mother—but I had no reason not to open the door. Maybe she was here seeking donations for the Cantors.

"Hi, Susan," I said, as I opened the door. "How are you?"

"Fine, thanks. How are *you*, Marcy?"

"I'm doing much better. Thanks for asking. What brings you by?" I asked.

"I brought her." Ed Harding had been standing at the side of the porch, just out of my range of vision. He now stepped up as Susan pushed her way into the house. After both she and Ed were inside, he closed the door.

"We want that tapestry," Ed continued. "Where is it?"

"I imagine it burned up in the Cantors' house yesterday," I said.

Ed shook his head. He was such a greasy, disagreeable old man—I had no clue what Susan saw in him.

"I went through that house top to bottom before I torched it," Ed said. "It wasn't there. So I figure either you've got it, or you know where it is."

"Why do you suddenly want the tapestry?" I asked. "Is it because of Explore Nation? If it is, you're out of luck. I've already spoken with Mr. Trammel and told him I thought the tapestry had burned up in the fire at the Cantors' house."

"We don't *suddenly* want the tapestry," Susan said. "We've wanted it since the first time you laid eyes on it, haven't we, Daddy?"

Daddy?

Ed nodded. "I never put any stock in Chester's belief that it was some kind of magical treasure map that would solve all his family's problems, but Susan said it was the only thing keeping that old man—and Mary—from moving out of the Cantors' house."

"Once she was gone, Adam would've seen how much better I'd be for him than Mary was," Susan said.

"Right," I said, my voice coming on the end of a sigh. There was no reasoning with her. If I was going to get out of this, I needed to appeal to Ed. "I'm sure if you turned yourself in, Mr. Harding, and explained that this was all an *accident* or something, then everything would work out all right in the end."

"Oh, it'll work out," he said. "But I'm not going to prison for arson."

I thought the arson charge would be the least of his worries after he was found guilty of the murder of Chester Cantor, but I continued to try to play dumb. "Susan, maybe if you talked with him. . . ."

"Nope," she said as breezily as if I'd asked her to try to change his mind about his restaurant preference. "I'm in too deep myself, at this point. Plus, Daddy and I decided that we'd never let each other down again, didn't we, Daddy?"

Ed nodded. "That's what we decided."

I had to do something. And I had to do it quickly.

"Um, look," I began. "I have some money in the kitchen—ten thousand dollars. I keep it hidden in there just in case."

Susan's eyes widened. "You keep ten thousand bucks in your kitchen?"

I nodded. "And it's yours if you'll just let me go."

Susan looked at Ed. He curved both sides of his mouth into a contemptible frown and gave a slight shake of his head.

"But don't think you could kill me and then find the money," I said. "You'd never find it if you didn't know exactly where to look."

Susan looked back at me.

"I'm offering you a way out," I said. "With that ten thousand dollars, you could make a nice nest egg for yourself, Adam, and Melanie."

Susan wanted to take me up on my offer. I could tell by the way she was biting her lip and looking anxiously from me to Ed.

"You can take the money, tie me to a kitchen chair, and then leave," I hurried on. "When Ted gets back—" I glanced at the hall clock. "Oh, goodness, he'll be back anytime—we need to hurry. Anyway, when he gets back, I'll tell him someone broke in and tied me up. I'll give him a fake description. The police will be looking for somebody else. Best of all, they won't be looking for two *murderers*."

"Come on, Daddy," Susan said. "What do you say? We really *could* use that ten thousand dollars to make a fresh start."

"Do you really trust her?" he asked.

She nodded. "Her mother is loaded. Works in the movie business."

"I don't mean do you trust her about the money. I'm asking if you honestly believe she'll keep her mouth shut about our coming here and robbing her?" he snarled. "Sometimes I can't believe how stupid you are."

"Stupid?" Susan sputtered. "*I'm* stupid? You're the one who jumped the gun and killed Chester

Cantor! And then you jumped the gun again and set the Cantors' house on fire! *I'm* the one who found you in that halfway house in Pennsylvania and gave you a life here."

"Some life!" he shouted.

"You have it a lot better than you *did*!"

As the two of them were arguing, I was backing ever so slowly toward the front door. Unfortunately, Ed noticed.

"Stop or I'll kill you right now!" he yelled at me.

I stopped.

"Show us where that money is," he said.

"Follow me." I headed for the kitchen. Although there was no money there, there were weapons. I just had to find one that would provide me the distraction I so desperately needed. The knives were too obvious; plus Ed would likely shoot me before I could get in the first jab.

The freezer. I'd heard once that people sometimes keep valuables in their freezers. As I walked, I did a speedy inventory of mine. I had a solidly frozen ham I meant to bake for Easter. And it was a big ham. I'd planned on having lots of guests if I wasn't able to spend the day with Mom. That might work.

I went to the freezer and opened it. I could feel Ed's hot, rancid breath on me. It made me feel nauseous. Well, that, and the prospect of imminent death.

"You keep ten grand in the freezer?" he asked.

"Yep. I like cold, hard cash."

"Ha-ha—"

Before he could finish that last "ha," I'd broadsided him in the face with the ham. He went down. Susan, who'd trailed along behind us, wailed, "Daddy!"

I threw the ham at her and raced out the back door. Angus came running, and he and I escaped through the gate. We hurried to my next-door neighbor's house, and I called nine-one-one.

Epilogue

By the time the police got to my house, Ed and Susan were gone. They didn't get far and were quickly caught, however, because they'd actually taken the time to go through my freezer to see if there was any money in it. As it was, everything in my freezer—including the ham—had been ruined. But, looking at the big picture, that was okay. Food could be replaced.

It turned out that Ed was Susan Willoughby's biological father. She'd always known she was adopted, and she'd been searching for her birth parents for years. When she'd found that her father was living in a halfway house in Pennsylvania, she'd sent for him and had been taking care of him for the past eight months. Why hadn't she introduced him around? The best Ted and I could come up with was that Susan was ashamed of him. She was trying to clean him up and find him some work before she let his identity be known. But Ed wasn't ready to give up his crooked ways and adapt himself to a more acceptable lifestyle.

Susan had been romantically interested in Adam Cantor, but Adam hadn't felt the same way about her. She'd hoped that by cultivating a friendship with Mary and having Ed cultivate a friendship with Chester, she could have excuses to be around Adam so he'd see what a great gal she was. He hadn't seen it. Adam *had* seen through Ed, though, and had refused to try to get him on with the company where he worked. He'd also discouraged his father from hanging around with Ed, so it was actually *Chester* who'd nixed the idea of their working together to find the treasure.

Speaking of the treasure—or, in this case, the tapestry—Adam had taken it to the dry cleaner after leaving my shop Saturday morning. He'd wanted it cleaned and preserved so he could frame it as a reminder of what his father had wanted for him and the rest of his family. Adam is on the road to recovery. He has enrolled in anger management classes and is seeing a therapist to help him resolve his abusive behavior. Contractors are working on their new house, and Melanie is excited that her new bedroom will have a window seat "perfect for doing embroidery, reading, or just daydreaming."

As for the reality show, it did go on. J. T. Trammel was "more tickled than a bedbug in a feather duster"—his words, not mine—that things turned out the way they did. He'd lined up one local who was willing to swear that the treasure of the *Delia* was cursed because it led to so much destruction. In spite of having a "cursed cargo," the sea did yield the *Delia*'s wreckage. So far, divers have recovered a handful of rare natural pearls. I'm thinking Melanie is going to have a fantastic college education!

Christine Willoughby started coming into the Seven-Year Stitch on a regular basis. During her last visit, she reported that Jared had been seeing "a sweet girl who works at MacKenzies' Mochas. Her name is Keira." To my credit, I kept my jaw from dropping to the floor, and I didn't let on to Christine that Keira was anything but "a sweet girl." Could Jared pick them, or what?

Remember how I'd been trying to get Audrey Dayton introduced to Todd? She took care of that herself. I saw her walking out of the Brew Crew with him at lunch the other day, and they were laughing. I hoped it would work out for them.

As for Ted and me, I finally got Mom's Easter egg finished. We went to spend Easter weekend with her in San Francisco and had a blast. It was Ted's first time in San Fran, and Mom and I had so much fun showing him the city.

So things were pretty much returning to normal. But then, this was Tallulah Falls. I knew I'd better enjoy it while it lasted.

AUTHOR'S NOTE

I had a lot of fun doing the research for this book. To learn about shipwrecks off the coast of Oregon, I consulted the following books:

- *Lost Treasure Ships of the Oregon Coast* by Theodore Schellhase
- *Peril at Sea: A Photographic Study of Shipwrecks in the Pacific* by Jim Gibbs
- *Guide to Shipwreck Sites Along the Oregon Coast* by Victor West
- *Buried Treasure of the Pacific Northwest* by W. C. Jameson

When I searched for these books, the *Guide to Shipwreck Sites Along the Oregon Coast* was out of print and came from a used bookseller. One of the book's previous owners had written notes in the margins, such as, "I remember going on this ship after it was on beach for some time. Still can see some remains." My grandmother used to write notes in the margins of books, and it made me treasure this little book all the more.

In addition to the books, I studied Web sites, including:

- Graveyard of the Pacific (http://historylink .org)
- Pacific Coast Pirates and Spanish Galleons (http://fncbooks.com/OregonPirates/)
- Oregon Coast Shipwrecks (http://www.theo regoncoast.info/Shipwrecks.html)
- Red Bubble (http://www.redbubble.com)
- Depoe Bay Annual Pirate Treasure Hunt (http://www.treasuredepoebay.org/)
- Pirates of the Pacific Festival (http://pirate softhepacificfestival.com/index.html)
- Underwater Archaeology (http://underwater archaeology.gr)
- Domestic Abuse Statistics (http://www.aard varc.org/) and (http://ncadv.org/)

Read on for a sneak peek
at another crafty Embroidery Mystery
from Amanda Lee

THE QUICK AND THE THREAD

Available from Obsidian.

Just after crossing over . . . under . . . through . . . the covered bridge, I could see it. Barely. I could make out the top of it, and that was enough at the moment to make me set aside the troubling grammatical conundrum of whether one passes over, under, or through a covered bridge.

"There it is," I told Angus, an Irish wolfhound who was riding shotgun. "There's our sign!"

He woofed, which could mean anything from "I gotta pee" to "Yay!" I went with "Yay!"

"Me, too! I'm so excited."

I was closer to the store now and could really see the sign. I pointed. "See, Angus?" My voice was barely above a whisper. "Our sign."

THE SEVEN-YEAR STITCH.

I had named the shop the Seven-Year Stitch for three reasons. One, it's an embroidery specialty shop. Two, I'm a huge fan of classic movies. And three, it actually took me seven years to turn my dream of owning an embroidery shop into a reality.

Once upon a time, in a funky-cool land called San Francisco, I was an accountant. Not a funky-cool job, believe me, especially for a funky-cool girl like me, Marcy Singer. I had a corner cubicle near a window. You'd think the window would be a good thing, but it looked out upon a vacant building that grew more dilapidated by the day. Maybe by the hour. It was majorly depressing. One year, a coworker gave me a cactus for my birthday. I set it in that window, and it died. I told you it was depressing.

Still, my job wasn't that bad. I can't say I truly enjoyed it, but I am good with numbers and the work was tolerable. Then I got the call from Sadie. Not a call, mind you; *the* call.

"Hey, Marce. Are you sitting down?" Sadie had said.

"Sadie, I'm always sitting down. I keep a stationary bike frame and pedal it under my desk so my leg muscles won't atrophy."

"Good. The hardware store next to me just went out of business."

"And this is good because you hate the hardware guy?"

She'd given me an exasperated huff. "No, silly. It's good because the space is for lease. I've already called the landlord, and he's giving you the opportunity to snatch it up before anyone else does."

Sadie is an entrepreneur. She and her husband, Blake, own MacKenzies' Mochas, a charming coffee shop on the Oregon coast. She thinks everyone—or, at least, Marcy Singer—should also own a charming shop on the Oregon coast.

"Wait, wait, wait," I'd said. "You expect me to come up there to Quaint City, Oregon—"

"Tallulah Falls, thank you very much."

"—and set up shop? Just like that?"

"Yes! It's not like you're happy there or like you're on some big five-year career plan."

"Thanks for reminding me."

"And you've not had a boyfriend or even a date for more than a year now. I could still strangle David when I think of how he broke your heart."

"Once again, thank you for the painful reminder."

"So what's keeping you there? This is your chance to open up the embroidery shop you used to talk about all the time in college."

"But what do I know about actually running a business?"

Sadie had huffed. "You can't tell me you've been keeping companies' books all these years without having picked up some pointers about how to—and how not to—run a business."

"You've got a point there. But what about Angus?"

"Marce, he will *love* it here! He can come to work with you every day, run up and down the beach. . . . Isn't that better than the situation he has now?"

I swallowed a lump of guilt the size of my fist.

"You're right, Sadie," I'd admitted. "A change will do us both good."

That had been three months ago. Now I was a resident of Tallulah Falls, Oregon, and today was the grand opening of the Seven-Year Stitch.

A cool, salty breeze off the ocean ruffled my hair as I hopped out of the bright red Jeep I'd bought to traipse up and down the coast.

Angus followed me out of the Jeep and trotted beside me up the river-rock steps to the walk that connected all the shops on this side of the street. The shops on the other side of the street were set up in a similar manner, with river-rock steps leading up to walks containing bits of shells and colorful rocks for aesthetic appeal. A narrow two-lane road divided the shops, and black wrought-iron lampposts and benches added to the inviting community feel. A large clock tower sat in the middle of the town square, pulling everything together and somehow reminding us all of the preciousness of time. Tallulah Falls billed itself as the friendliest town on the Oregon coast, and so far, I had no reason to doubt that claim.

I unlocked the door and flipped the closed sign to open before turning to survey the shop. It was as if I were seeing it for the first time. And, in a way, I was. I'd been here until nearly midnight last night, putting the finishing touches on everything. This was my first look at the finished project. Like all my finished projects, I tried to view it objectively. But, like all my finished projects, I looked upon this one as a cherished child.

The floor was black-and-white tile laid out like a gleaming chessboard. All my wood accents were maple. On the floor to my left, I had maple bins holding cross-stitch threads and yarns. When a customer first came in the door, she would see the cross-stitch threads. They started in white and went through shades of ecru, pink, red, orange, yellow, green, blue, purple, gray, and black. The yarns were organized the same way on the opposite side. Perle flosses, embroidery hoops, needles, and cross-stitch kits hung on maple-trimmed corkboard over the bins. On the other side of the corkboard—the side with the yarn—there were knitting needles, crochet hooks, tapestry needles, and needlepoint kits.

The walls were covered by shelves where I displayed pattern books, dolls with dresses I'd designed and embroidered, and framed samplers. I had some dolls for those who liked to sew and embroider outfits (like me), as well as for those who enjoyed knitting and crocheting doll clothes.

Standing near the cash register was my life-size mannequin, who bore a striking resemblance to

Marilyn Monroe, especially since I put a short, curly blond wig on her and did her makeup. I even gave her a mole . . . er, beauty mark. I called her Jill. I was going to name her after Marilyn's character in *The Seven Year Itch*, but she didn't have a name. Can you believe that—a main character with no name? She was simply billed as "The Girl."

To the right of the door was the sitting area. As much as I loved to play with the amazing materials displayed all over the store, the sitting area was my favorite place in the shop. Two navy overstuffed sofas faced each other across an oval maple coffee table. The table sat on a navy, red, and white braided rug. There were red club chairs with matching ottomans near either end of the coffee table, and candlewick pillows with lace borders scattered over both the sofas. I made those, too—the pillows, not the sofas.

The bell over the door jingled, and I turned to see Sadie walking in with a travel coffee mug.

I smiled. "Is that what I think it is?"

"It is, if you think it's a nonfat vanilla latte with a hint of cinnamon." She handed me the mug. "Welcome to the neighborhood."

"Thanks. You're the best." The steaming mug felt good in my hands. I looked back over the store. "It looks good, doesn't it?"

"It looks fantastic. You've outdone yourself." She

cocked her head. "Is that what you're wearing to-night?"

Happily married for the past five years, Sadie was always eager to play matchmaker for me. I hid a smile and held the hem of my vintage tee as if it were a dress. "You don't think Snoopy's Joe Cool is appropriate for the grand opening party?"

Sadie closed her eyes.

"I have a supercute dress for tonight," I said with a laugh, "and Mr. O'Ruff will be sporting a black tie for the momentous event."

Angus wagged his tail at the sound of his sur-name.

"Marce, you and that *pony*." Sadie scratched An-gus behind the ears.

"He's a proud boy. Aren't you, Angus?"

Angus barked his agreement, and Sadie chuckled.

"I'm proud, too . . . of both of you." She grinned. "I'd better get back over to Blake. I'll be back to check on you again in a while."

Though we're the same age and had been room-mates in college, Sadie clucked over me like a mother hen. It was sweet, but I could do without the fix-ups. Some of these guys she'd tried to foist on me . . . I have no idea where she got them—mainly because I was afraid to ask.

I went over to the counter and placed my big yellow purse and floral tote bag on the bottom shelf before finally taking a sip of my latte.

"That's yummy, Angus. It's nice to have a friend who owns a coffee shop, isn't it?"

Angus lay down on the large bed I'd put behind the counter for him.

"That's a good idea," I told him. "Rest up. We've got a big day and an even bigger night ahead of us."

At about ten a.m., a woman wearing a smart black pantsuit, a paisley scarf, and bold silver jewelry entered the shop. *My first customer*. I caught my breath when I saw that she was holding a list.

"Good morning," I said. "Welcome to the Seven-Year Stitch. I'm Marcy Singer. May I help you find anything?"

The woman smiled. "I'm working on a cross-stitch piece for my granddaughter, and I need some metallic threads, beads, and ribbon to finish it. Everything is written down here." She handed me the list.

I was relieved to see that I had in stock everything she needed. I invited her to take a look around the shop, or to take a seat in the sitting area while I gathered her items.

"I'm having an open house tonight, if you'd like

to stop by," I said as I put skeins of metallic thread into a shopping basket. "It's just a drop-in event—nothing fancy."

"I'll try to stop by," she said. "This is really a lovely shop."

I couldn't help feeling a burst of pride. "Thanks. It certainly doesn't appear that you need lessons yourself, but if you know anyone who'd be interested, I have sign-up sheets for crewel, cross-stitch, and candlewick classes—beginning and advanced—on the counter."

"Oh, I've always wanted to learn to do crewel." She stood and walked to the counter. "I'll sign up for that one, and my friend Martha might be interested, as well."

"Terrific." I returned to the counter with all the items on her list.

"I'm Sarah Crenshaw, by the way."

"Sarah, it's a pleasure to meet you. You're my first customer, and as such, I'd like to offer you a ten-percent discount," I said in my best professional-shopkeeper voice.

Well, now I knew there was one sure way to put a smile on my customers' faces.

As she left, I called, "I hope to see you this evening."

"I'll see what I can do."

When she was out of sight, I dropped to the floor and hugged Angus. "Our cash register has actual cash in it!"

He wagged his tail.

The rest of the day passed quickly. Some Tallulah Falls residents stopped by to wish me well; many bought threads, patterns, and fabrics, and most promised to return for the evening's festivities. Sadie and Blake had enjoyed a busy day next door at MacKenzies' Mochas, too, but Sadie had still managed to stop in for a quick hello after the lunch rush.

I closed the shop and hurried home to get ready. I had an actual house here, as opposed to the apartment I had in San Francisco. I bought the house shortly after leasing the shop, and I had finally finished unpacking the past weekend. Of course, in San Fran, I spent a lot of time at Mom's house, too, which was okay, but that doesn't lend itself to a mature, independent lifestyle.

I liked being a homeowner. Sadie said it was because nothing had been broken yet, but I was optimistic. I'm not bragging, but my two-story house was gorgeous . . . especially compared to the cramped little apartment I had overlooking the San Francisco Bay. Here, while I didn't have a direct view of the ocean, I could hear it all the time. It was wonderfully serene. I was also within walking distance of the beach, which was great, because Angus seemed to adore romping along the shore.

I went upstairs to get ready. I showered, dried my hair, and then padded into the bedroom to get dressed. I opened the closet and took out my black lace dress. I slipped the dress over my head and smoothed the material over my hips. The dress came to just above my knees, but it didn't do much to make me look taller. Maybe the four-inch-high red stilettos would help. The black did make my pale skin and platinum hair stand out, especially with my splash of red lipstick. I was going for an Old Hollywood look, and I thought I was pulling if off rather well.

My mind drifted back to Mom as I dug through my jewelry box for my pair of jet beaded chandelier earrings I love so much. You could say Angus and I had gone and loaded up the truck and moved to Beverly. But actually, we'd moved *away* from Beverly—Singer, that is, aka Mom, movie-costume designer extraordinaire.

I gave myself a mental shake. Why in the world was I thinking about *The Beverly Hillbillies* theme song? Of course, thinking about *The Beverly Hillbillies* brought Buddy Ebsen to mind. And that, in turn, made me remember he'd played Audrey Hepburn's estranged husband in *Breakfast at Tiffany's*. Random trivia seems to be always lurking just beneath the surface of my mind.

I took a long black cigarette holder from inside my jewelry box and placed it between my teeth. Mom had given it to me years ago. It had been a prop on some movie set. God only knew who had used it, so she'd insisted on scalding it before giving it to me. Good thing. While I've never been a smoker, I used to love pretending to use the long black cigarette holder. It made me remember how even Lucille Ball as Lucy Ricardo had used one to make her look sophisticated after she and Ethel had attended charm school.

I sighed. Leaving Mom behind in San Francisco had been the one drawback to my moving to Tallulah Falls. I wished Mom could have made the party, but she was in New York on a movie set. It was par for the course. In many ways, I grew up privileged. But I was lonely for my mother, who was often on location somewhere, and since Dad had died when I was very young, I'd often been left in the care of my nanny.

I have to give Mom credit for passing along to me my love of textiles, though. When she was home, Mom often allowed me to come to the studio and help work with the fabrics. She'd wanted me to go into fashion and costume design. A rebellious little snot at the time, I'd told her I wanted a "more stable and reliable" career. Mom said I'd be bored with a reliable career. While I'd admitted that accounting wouldn't be as exciting as dressing Hollywood's A-listers, I asserted that it would allow me to be home for my family, should I ever be fortunate enough to have one. I told you I was a rebellious little snot. That comment had hurt Mom. And I'd meant it to. At the time, I wouldn't have taken it back for anything in the world, even if I could have. Now that I was a wee bit older and wiser, I regretted it.

During my rebellious late-teen years, I even stopped going to Mom's studio. It was like I was spiting her, but I was really hurting only myself. I hadn't realized that until I was in college. I'd come back to the dorm one evening to find Sadie laboriously trying to embroider a pair of jeans. I took over the task and rediscovered my love for the craft. Still, I was too proud to admit that to Mom, so I'd sucked it up and embarked on my career in accounting.

I found the chandelier earrings I'd been looking for and put them on. Taking one last imaginary puff from the cigarette holder, I placed it back in the jewelry box.

I called Angus to me and put his black bow tie around his neck. Then I batted my lashes at him and imitated Bette Davis: "Fasten your seat belts. It's going to be a bumpy night."

ABOUT THE AUTHOR

Amanda Lee lives in southwest Virginia with her husband and two beautiful children, a boy and a girl. She's a full-time writer/editor/mom/wife and chief cook and bottle washer, and she loves every minute of it. Okay, not the bottle washing so much, but the rest of it is great.

CONNECT ONLINE

www.gayletrent.com
www.facebook.com/gayletrentandamandalee
twitter.com/gayletrent

Melissa Bourbon

Deadly Patterns
A Magical Dressmaking Mystery

Bliss, Texas, is gearing up for its annual Winter
Wonderland spectacular and Harlow is planning the main
event: a holiday fashion show being held at an old
Victorian mansion. But when someone is found dead on
the mansion's grounds, it's up to Harlow to catch the
killer—before she becomes a suspect herself.

**"Harlow Jane Cassidy is a
tailor-made amateur sleuth."
—Wendy Lyn Watson**

<u>Also available in the series</u>
A Fitting End
Pleating for Mercy

Available wherever books are sold or at
penguin.com

facebook.com/TheCrimeSceneBooks

Sally Goldenbaum

DEATH BY CASHMERE
A Seaside Knitters Mystery

Isabel "Izzy" Chambers raises some eyebrows when she rents the apartment above her yarn shop to Angie Archer, whose reputation has made her unpopular with many locals. But could any of them have wanted her dead?

When Angie's body is discovered drowned in the harbor, an official investigation rules the death an accident. There are speculations of too many whiskey sours, a slippery wharf, a dark night. But Izzy and the Seaside Knitters smell something fishy. When several strange incidents occur above the shop, the women decide to take matters into their own hands. But before long, their small-town sense of security is frayed, and the threat of more violence hangs over this tightly knit community.

Also Available
Patterns in the Sand
Moon Spinners
A Holiday Yarn
The Wedding Shawl
A Fatal Fleece

Available wherever books are sold or at
penguin.com